MW00943300

"An intriguing novel about the birth of the motion picture industry, as seen through the eyes of a young man striving to strike it big. The novel's historical setting comes to life with detailed references to 1910s Hollywood, from the intensive artwork of Griffith's sets to the lower-budget yet groundbreaking work of actors such as Charlie Chaplin and producers such as Noble Johnson, founder of the Lincoln Motion Picture Company. [The novel's] rich detail and the mystery of Jimmy's mother's disappearance make for an engrossing read."

— *Kirkus Reviews*

"Joseph M. Humbert's fresh and absorbing new historical novel explores the distinctions between white and black filmmaking of the time, side-by-side with the larger conflicts between white and black life in America. He handles his topic with a light and engaging touch, but always with an underlying sense of historical gravitas. Will Jimmy succeed in cinema? Will he resolve his recurring nightmare about the disappearance of his mother? Will he etch out a life of achievement and dignity in an early-20th-century environment of prejudice, chauvinism, and bigotry? This is the story that Joseph Humbert tells in *There's the Rub,* a thoughtful, moving, and stellar first novel."

— *Rossmoor News*

"*There's the Rub* is an interesting story about life in the entertainment industry when motion pictures were new and racism was pervasive. Through the story of the Johnson family, author Joseph M. Humbert aptly depicts a time that was both exciting and hopeful, but also relentlessly unjust. Readers will appreciate the skillful way the author has blended his fictional characters into a backdrop of historical fact, introducing a cast of real-life figures, such as film director D. W. Griffith, actor Noble Johnson, and actress Madame Sul-te-wan."

— *ForeWord Clarion Reviews*

THERE'S THE RUB

BY
JOSEPH M. HUMBERT

Cover art by Hizuru Cruz
Author photo by David Humbert

CreateSpace Independent Publishing Platform
North Charleston, SC

*For my loving wife,
Bernice, and our two sons,
Michael and David*

"The past is a foreign country: they
do things differently there."

— L. P. Hartley

HOLLYWOOD 1916

The Babylonian set
in D.W. Griffith's
Intolerance

Noble Johnson and
The Lincoln Motion
Picture Company

Madame Sul-te-Wan

TABLE OF CONTENTS

THERE'S THE RUB

CHAPTER 1

PERCHANCE
TO DREAM

Hollywood, California (1915).   At first light, Jimmy Johnson woke up with a start. Was it the dream again? For much of his twenty-six years, Jimmy, a grandson of slaves, had been haunted by a recurring dream—a nightmare really. It started shortly after his mother had seemingly abandoned him, his younger brother, and their father. He had been only five at the time. Why would she do that? Why would any mother do that?

But did she really abandon them? The dream suggested otherwise. His memory of the events of that terrible night was murky, made less reliable by the reinforcing nature of dreams. What was real? What was imagined? His father, Reed, knew more than he wanted to tell. He only said that she was an unfit mother. If she really abandoned them without explanation, then he was right. But again, the dream and his memory suggested otherwise.

He couldn't get it out of his craw that maybe her leaving was his fault. He remembered trying hard to please his father. Did this effort drive away his mother? But how could a five-year-old do that? Except now, he had also displeased his father; so much so that his father had for all intents and purposes disowned him. He had no contact with his father or his younger brother, Russell, for the past six years.

While he had mixed feelings about his father, Jimmy did miss his brother. In the fifteen years of growing up together without their mother, they may have formed a stronger bond than if their mother was still around. Hell, Jimmy still owed Russell fifty dollars and wanted to repay him as he had promised. But with Reed and Russell always on the road with their vaudeville act, it was impossible to catch up with them. Jimmy was on the West Coast while they were traveling the vaudeville theaters of the Chitlin' Circuit. These theaters catered to colored audiences east of the Mississippi River, across the top of the Midwest, down the Eastern seaboard, through the Deep South, and back up the Mississippi. Reed and Russell were 'Johnson and Son,' a tap dancing duet.

A more daunting task for Jimmy was his effort to find his mother. If he could find her, he could ask her what had happened that terrible night, not to lay blame, but to get to the truth, and maybe, just maybe, prevent that damned nightmare from invading his brain. To that end, Jimmy had spent a good deal of time trying to track down Miriam Johnson. Over the years, there were so many false leads, so many dead ends. It was as if she had vanished from this earth. Perhaps she had died but he refused to think that. Don't ask him why but he just knew she was out there, somewhere. He hadn't yet given up hope.

Thinking about it, maybe the dream was not what had given him such a fitful night. Yesterday, he saw D. W. Griffith's epic, *The Birth of a Nation*, at a movie theater downtown. He was one of a handful of coloreds segregated to the balcony, derisively called the buzzard's roost, or crow's nest. He heard all the talk but he just had to see this moving picture for himself. What did this white man—this D. W. Griffith—have to say about his family?

In the theater, while Jimmy was gripped by Griffith's storytelling powers in this new and exciting medium, his blood boiled over the story. Towards the end, when men in hooded sheets rode on horses to rescue beleaguered Southerners, some audience members stood up, cheered, whooped, and hollered. That did it.

Jimmy stood up, too. He pointed to the screen and yelled, "Go to Hell, D. W. Griffith!" It was as much to the cheering audience as to the flickering images. Reactions from the audience below ranged from jeers to support.

"Who's that?"

"Some nigger upstairs."

"Go back to Africa!"

"Leave him alone."

"He's right, dammit."

"Shut up!"

Jimmy stormed out. A few other audience members did too, not all of them people of color.

Outside the theater, Jimmy walked past a long line of theater goers waiting for the next show. He barely noticed them as he was deep in thought.

By this morning, it had come to him. With his job fixing cameras in downtown Hollywood, he had come to learn about movie equipment. He always had a knack for fixing things. Even as a kid, he would take things apart and put them back together, like the time when he tried to fix his father's pocket watch. When he couldn't get the face cover back on, his father was not happy, in fact, he was furious. And he and Russell learned early on that you don't want to make Reed unhappy. Reed took the watch to a proper watch repairman. He vowed never again to let Jimmy touch it.

In delivering repaired cameras and film stock to the studios of the burgeoning silent movie industry in Los Angeles, Jimmy managed to steal a few minutes to watch them make moving pictures. It did not seem hard. On that morning, he decided that he too would learn the process, and make pictures that did not do violence to his family. How he hated D. W. Griffith. Within a year, in Hollywood, in the spring of 1916, Jimmy would be finishing his first one-reel photoplay.

LEAVING HOME

Memphis, Tennessee (1865). On a day in mid-May, Jimmy's grandfather and namesake, James Johnson, had tears of joy and sadness. Joy as he held his newborn son who his wife, Lethe, had just delivered. They named him Reed. He had such a strong voice, this young'un. But James' heart ached because he had learned that day that a damned Southerner actor had assassinated his beloved President, Abraham Lincoln, the month before. James and his wife were free from the bonds of their owners because of Mr. Lincoln. With the Civil War just over, they had much hope for the future. Now, with Mr. Lincoln gone, there was much uncertainty, not only for their own lives but for the country.

James and Lethe had been owned by the Johnson family on a plantation near Nashville. After emancipation, James and Lethe were offered to work as sharecroppers for Mr. Johnson but they chose instead to find their future in Memphis, a town where they had heard many freed slaves found work.

On the morning of their departure in late October 1864, James and Lethe packed for the 200 miles trek west. After saying "good-bye" to those who chose to stay behind, James and Lethe started their journey. On their way out, they visited their parents' final resting spot, in the burying-ground of slaves. The morning air was crisp as winter was approaching. They crunched through fallen dried poplar leaves. Four large stones marked the graves. They both wept, knowing they may never come back again. James got on his knees, closed his eyes, and bowed his head. He clasped his hands together in prayer. Standing behind her husband, and fighting tears, Lethe said haltingly, "Mother, Father—and mother, father to James—we leave you now... and bless you." She rubbed her slightly bulging abdomen, and continued, "But know that your grandchild and their children's children will not... will not be born as slaves." With that, they began their eight day journey.

At first, it was hard finding work in Memphis that winter but work did come. James worked at odd jobs while Lethe found work cleaning houses. Just before their first Christmas in Memphis, James saw many people crowding around the newspaper office which posted their front page in the window. People were talking about how the damned Yankees had crushed the Confederate Army of Tennessee in Nashville. The fact that Negro troops helped in the defeat brought a smile to James' face.

Just before Reed's first birthday, James and Lethe questioned their move from the plantation. A year after the War had ended, the pain of defeat left raw nerves in the South. A race riot exploded in town and encroached on the neighborhood of freed slaves where they lived. On that first night, when white townspeople brought torches, a fearful Lethe grabbed the baby and wrapped him in a quilt she made. She took some food and begged James to come with her. Wanting at first to stay and protect their home, James quickly realized that she was right. He grabbed more food and they both ran out the back door just as a brick shattered their front window.

They found refuge near the Mississippi and stayed hidden for three days until Federal troops came in and stopped the rioting. When they returned, several of their neighbors had been killed or their homes burned or robbed. Their home was not burned but was looted. Lethe looked around their home and cried. What little possessions they had was either gone or destroyed. James hugged her. Just then, baby Reed cooed. James and Lethe looked at their son, then at each other and smiled. They realized what was important and what wasn't. In the aftermath of those terrible three days, an uneasy peace had come over the city. James and Lethe decided to stay and help with their neighbors to rebuild.

James ended up working at a barber shop and learned how to cut hair. After a few years he and Lethe were able to save enough to open their own barber shop. One of the first things that James bought with the first week's proceeds was a pocket watch, a watch that he treasured for much of his life.

Every Sunday in church, youngster Reed would sing in the children's choir and attend Sunday school. Much to the displeasure of his parents, Reed wasn't much for book learning. Although a slave on the plantation, James was taught to read and to sum by a kindly preacher, a dangerous activity since this was illegal in the South. He and his wife valued education. They tried to pass this value to their young son but the boy had too much nervous energy to sit properly in a schoolhouse. The school teacher explained that Reed would sometimes just leave in the middle of lessons and not return. James and Lethe tried their best to teach Reed at home but they never had proper schooling themselves and they needed to spend many long hours at the barber shop. At the shop, young Reed would help them, sweeping floors and washing towels. James tried to teach him hair cutting but Reed did not have the patience and James had to fix his mistakes on unhappy customers and not charge them.

Reed found that he had a natural talent for dance. Whenever he heard music, he had to move his feet. As his dancing brought accolades and praise from customers in the shop, he was emboldened to do more. James would good-naturedly admonish his customers by saying, "Don't encourage the boy." He was only half kidding.

Outside of a vaudeville theater in town, teenager Reed was practicing his steps to music in his head. One tap dance performer on the bill, Edgar Perry, a few years older than Reed, was leaving the theater after a matinee and happened to see him practicing. He immediately recognized the talent of this young man and struck up a conversation.

"Man, that sure is fancy footwork," Edgar said.

Reed slowed down and stopped. "Thanks, mister. Say, aren't you Edgar Perry?"

Edgar gave a deep bow.

"I seen your name on the bill."

"How old are you, uh...?"

"Reed, Reed Johnson. Eighteen, come May."

"Who taught you those steps?" He laughed, "Boz's Juba?"

Reed had never heard of the black man who dazzled white audiences in the United States and London nearly half a century before with his new style of dance. Even Charles Dickens wrote about him in his *American Notes*. Reed said, "I teached myself."

Edgar whistled in amazement. "Listen, kid, ever think of taking those feet on the road? I'm actually looking for a partner. You game?"

Reed's eyes lit up. He thought, "Imagine, me with Edgar Perry." Visions of fame, fortune, and getting out of this town filled Reed's head. He said, "I'll have to talk to my ma and pa first."

"Well, Reed Johnson, what are we waiting for?"

Reed's parents were skeptical at first. Who was this Edgar Perry fellow that wanted to "steal" their boy? Sure, they had heard of him but who was he really? They had hoped that Reed would do the sensible thing and follow in his father's footsteps, that is, take over the barber shop. In the end they realized that that wasn't going to happen. Reed did not have the wherewithal to properly run a business like the barber shop, at least, not yet. They slowly came around to realize that just as they had to leave the plantation to find their way in Memphis, Reed would have to leave Memphis to find his way in the world outside of Tennessee. Edgar asked them to give Reed a chance to prove himself. In the end, James and Lethe warily approved.

Over the next two weeks in Memphis, Edgar honed the rough talent of Reed into part of a cohesive two-man act. Reed had a lot to learn but the one lesson from his parents that stuck was not to be afraid of hard work. He didn't know it but this opportunity was thing he had been waiting for. They gave a preview of their new act at the vaudeville theater in Memphis with James, Lethe, friends, and neighbors attending. They were duly impressed and gave 'Perry and Johnson and Their Feets of Magic' a wild ovation. Reed was all smiles. He fed off that adoration like a drunk over whiskey—he yearned for more.

However, Reed had some trepidation as he packed to go on a long journey with Edgar. They would be gone for six months, going to places like Chicago, Detroit, New York, Philadelphia, Washington, D.C., Baltimore, Richmond, and Jacksonville. At the train station, there was much excitement and much sadness as he and his mother and father waited for Edgar. Finally, Edgar arrived with his suitcase. He wore a heavy overcoat and a derby hat.

Reed pointed, and remarked, "Nice hat."

Edgar took it off and admired it. "We can use it in our act. We'll get one for you in Chicago." They turned when they heard a distant train whistle and looked down the tracks. It was the 7:15 for Chicago.

Edgar pointed, and said, "Thar she blows, matey." He picked up his suitcase.

Lethe's eyes were starting to well up and she took out a handkerchief. Reed saw this and said, "Ma, it's going to be all right."

She smiled, and said, "I know. I know." The huge iron beast passed them as it slowed up and stopped, releasing a huge plume of steam, the hissing sound of it was as loud as the amount of the enveloping vapor. Conductors opened the doors, stepped out, and helped passengers disembark. Edgar, having done this a hundred times before, ran to get on board. He looked behind at the Johnson family, let out a loud whistle, and then yelled, "Come on, Reed."

Reed took a deep breath and picked up his suitcase. At the last minute, James took out his pocket watch and gave it to Reed. "Here, son, you take it."

Reed was stunned, "But, Pa, this is your watch."

"I want you to have it. You're a man now."

Reed's eyes teared up as he took the watch and pocketed it. He knew this was his father's most prized possession. "I said I wasn't going to cry. I'll take care of it, Pa, I promise."

"I know you will." He hugged his son. Reed hugged his mother who kissed him on the cheek. He said to her, "I'll write." She smiled, knowing he had all the best intentions. Edgar whistled one more time and Reed picked up his suitcase and got on the train with Edgar. Later, as the train began to move, James watched Lethe walk along side the train waving to her son. She stopped, and she and James went home to a house made emptier. A new reality, it would be the first time in nearly twenty years that they wouldn't have Reed around.

The train car that Edgar and Reed settled in was vacant and they sat in the back. While Reed looked out the window at the passing scenery, Edgar put his hat over his eyes to get some sleep. With stops along the way, more and more passengers—whites and coloreds—got on. Generally, both races rode in the second class cars together in the Northern and Western states without incident. For the railroads, even though the barons may have preferred segregation, it was economically infeasible to provide two separate cars for the races, with the extra weight and fuel costs. However, once Edgar and Reed crossed below the Mason-Dixon line, things were much different. The barons had to accede to the politics of the region.

At a stop, two white passengers got on their car with a conductor. The car was otherwise full. Edgar saw what has happening and rolled his eyes. The conductor approached the men, and said, "Time to git." Edgar took a deep breath, got up and grabbed his derby that he put on with aplomb. He looked at his partner and said, "Come on, Reed."

Reed looked out the window at the station name, and said, "What for? This ain't our stop."

"NOW!"

Not understanding but obeying, Reed followed Edgar and the conductor off the car. The conductor pointed to the front of the train to a car right behind the tender, commonly called the Jim Crow car. It was partitioned into three sections, one for colored, one for whites with baggage between them. They boarded the colored section. It was filled with other black passengers, men and women, as well as cigarette smoke. And, they had to stand. Reed just stared at his second class ticket and shook his head. Edgar explained with anger in his eyes, "It is what it is. I seen guys like us get thrown off the train for putting up a fuss. And the frickin' train didn't even slow down!" Reed put away his ticket and sighed.

While enduring these indignities, Reed, still in his teens, was feeling untethered and homesick. However he didn't let Edgar know or let his discomfort interfere with his work. Slowly, his longing for Memphis faded as he savored each new city, each new experience. He couldn't have fathomed that places like Chicago or New York even existed. With each new stop, true to his word, he would write a letter or send a postcard. Of course, he couldn't receive any mail as he was constantly on the move. He struggled with his writing. He now wished he had paid more attention in school as his parents had wanted. On one card, he wrote:

"Hello Ma and Pa. Its a beautyful day now. The train got here in the middle of the nite. It was raney hard. We stade in the station untell the rane stopt. We lade down on the benches. Boy, they were hard. Onley now, we are in a hotel room. Our first show is tonite. Miss you. Your lovin son, Reed."

Lethe and James were always excited to receive mail from their boy. Since Lethe couldn't read, James read the postcards and letters to his wife. He pretended it was his fault when he struggled through Reed's misspellings.

Just as Reed's parents had feared, Edgar introduced Reed to some of the more unsavory aspects of life, like drink and what they called fallen women. Reed had never once considered visiting the whorehouses in Memphis but Edgar had no qualms about introducing the boy to the pleasures of the flesh.

When Reed and Edgar made it back to the Memphis after that first tour, James and Lethe were overjoyed in seeing their son again. Lethe showed him all the postcards and letters she received. She and his father marveled at all the places he visited that they only heard about. But they saw too how much he had changed, how much he had matured in so little time. They were happy that Edgar did not take outward advantage of him, and had brought their son home in good health. And Reed still had his father's pocket watch, in good working order.

Over the next few years, Reed's parents became proud that 'Perry and Johnson and Their Feets of Magic' had become well known. At the barber shop James even displayed a playbill from a Harlem vaudeville theater showing his son's act as top billing. Whenever Reed and Edgar made it back into town, they were quite the conversation piece.

CHAPTER 3

A CHANCE MEETING CHANGES ALL

I n the 1880s, Edgar and Reed were living life to the fullest. It was not always carefree but they more than managed to get by. And they became the best of friends. They were two young men with no responsibilities except to be at the theater on time. The world started to open up for them.

One day, Edgar came into their hotel room whistling. Reed was lying down on his bed catching on up some sleep. Edgar woke him up.

"Hey, buddy boy."

Without opening his eyes, Reed said, "Let me sleep. You know how late we came in last night."

Edgar shook him more. "I got some fantastic news."

Reed reluctantly lifted himself up on one elbow and yawned. "Well..."

"Do you know who I was talking to?"

Reed grimaced and said, "I'm a hoofer, man, not a mind reader." He laid back down, covering his eyes with his right arm.

Edgar sat down on his bed and started to take off his shoes. "Robert Goodwin."

"Who?"

"Goodwin—he's that big promoter from the East Coast. He likes what we do. If we play our cards right, we could be downtown on Broadway in New York!"

Reed looked at Edgar and laughed, "Two guys like us? That's what I like about you, Edgar. Always thinking ahead." He closed his eyes again. "Wake me when it happens."

Edgar said, "If Boz's Juba can do it, so can we." He threw a pillow at Reed.

Their friendship lasted five years and it might have lasted longer if it weren't for one thing—they met seventeen-year-old Miriam Hopkins. Miriam was in a vaudeville act with her father, Bailey, and mother, Etta, called 'The Hopkins Trio.' Miriam was beautiful and talented. Both men were smitten by her. She was naturally kept on a short leash by her parents, so it took a while for either man to get close to her, especially when the acts did not play the same cities at the same time.

At first, the play for Miriam was like a game—it was for fun. One time Miriam acted like she liked Edgar, then she would like Reed. Each would serenade her, bringing her flowers or small gifts. Reed was first to recognize that to get to Miriam, he would have to get to her parents. When they all happened to be playing in Memphis the next time, Reed got his father to give Bailey a free haircut and for the families to meet. He even arranged for a Sunday picnic in the park.

This was unbeknownst to Edgar who woke up late on that Sunday morning. Reed was gone but he expected that. Although Reed was a regular churchgoer before he met Edgar, he never attended church on the road. But whenever they made it back to Memphis, Reed dutifully went to church with his parents. Edgar took a leisurely breakfast at a diner he frequented when in town. Satisfied and feeling pretty good, and not having to perform again until the evening, Edgar decided to call on Miriam. He bought a bouquet of flowers thinking he could woo Miriam in going on a walk with him. He got to the hotel where she and her parents were staying and knocked on their door. No answer. He went downstairs to the front desk, and asked the clerk, "Pardon me, my good man, any word about the Hopkins family in 310?"

The clerk answered, "They left earlier to take a stroll on the river."

"Thank you." Edgar flipped a quarter to the man. "Perfect," Edgar thought. There was one area of the Mississippi that was particularly suited for that. He whistled as he headed out the door.

At a grassy knoll overlooking the now peaceful river, Edgar's smile faded and his walk slowed down when he found the Hopkins family. They were picnicking with Reed and his parents, all still in their Sunday best. Before he saw them, he tossed the flowers aside and considered turning about. "Nah," he thought, "I'm not gonna to let Reed take this one without a say-so." He strode into their midst.

Looking up, Reed nearly choked on a biscuit, "Edgar!"

All others looked up. Miriam felt apprehension as the parents unknowingly smiled.

Edgar said, "Well, lookie, lookie, lookie." A pause. "Good morning, all. A beautiful day for a picnic."

All acknowledged. Edgar continued, "I was just taking a stroll and saw my favorite people."

Reed stood up, unsure of what to do. "Edgar... Won't you join us?" Miriam looked at him as if wondering whether this was the right thing to do.

Reed moved over to create a space away from Miriam but Edgar forced him the other way so that he could be between

Miriam and Reed. Now, the parents sensed trouble. They offered lunch, "How about some chicken, or potato salad?"

"Don't mind if I do." He took a drumstick and started eating it. "Hmm. Delicious."

James asked, "How are you enjoying your stay in Memphis?"

"I always have a special fondness for this town. After all, it's where I found... Reed." He punched Reed on a shoulder but with a bit more force than Reed would have liked. Edgar turned to Reed, "You didn't tell me you were going on a picnic."

Reed played dumb, "Didn't I? I thought I did."

Edgar wrapped his arm around Reed and squeezed him hard. "No, you didn't, buddy boy, my partner who didn't know a thing about stage performin' until I showed him. He'd still be stuck here hoofin' for pennies on the sidewalk if it weren't for me," Edgar said, smiling sardonically.

They all saw what was happening. Reed's father, James, stood up, as did Bailey. James said, "Sir, I believe it's time for you to take your leave."

Edgar's attitude turned sour. He released Reed, and then stood up, throwing his unfinished drumstick down, splattering in the bowl of potato salad. The two mothers gasped at this turn of events. Edgar said angrily, "All right. I don't want to spoil your precious little picnic. Eat. Eat!"

Edgar turned and walked away. The tension in the group subsided but they watched anxiously as Reed got up, ran after Edgar and caught up with him. Because Reed and Edgar were about twenty feet away the group couldn't exactly hear what was said but things didn't seem to get better. Edgar put a menacing finger into Reed's face and stomped away much angrier. Reed just took a deep breath and came back to the group. "Sorry about that."

"Will he be okay?" Lethe asked.

"Oh, yeah. He just needs to walk it off." He then smiled, reached down, and pulled Miriam up. Knowing what was to happen, Miriam looked demure and smiled too. Holding her hand, Reed said, "We're not going to let Edgar spoil this. With you all here, Miriam and I would like to announce..." He took a deep breath, "...our plans to get married."

All the parents were pleased. They stood up and hugged the newlyweds to be. The two future father-in-laws shook hands.

"This is wonderful."

"Congratulations."

"We couldn't be happier."

Neither could Miriam and Reed. Even though Reed said that things with Edgar would be all right, he knew it was a lie. Although they performed that night, it was the beginning of the end. Backstage, at the end of the show, Reed broke the news to Edgar about the wedding plans. Not only that, he was quitting the act with Edgar and forming a new act with Miriam. With fire in his eyes, Edgar stormed out of the theater. They would not perform together again. Edgar disappeared for three days, causing the cancelation of their last three shows.

Six months later, Reed and Miriam were getting ready to be married in the spacious and neatly groomed back yard of James and Lethe's home in Memphis. Miriam's parents were there as were friends and relatives. All were dressed in their Sunday best. The leaves on the trees were getting their autumn colors. Though invited out of respect, Edgar was conspicuously absent. Reed and Miriam were not surprised and somewhat relieved.

It couldn't have been a lovelier day as the happy couple stood facing each other with the minister of the Johnson's church officiating. As the minister started to speak, a lone clapping began behind the seated attendees. All turned to see Edgar. Reed's stomach fell. Intoxicated, unshaven, Edgar took a swig from the whiskey flask he was holding. This drew much murmur from the crowd. Those in the wedding party looked concerned.

Edgar slurred his words as he stumbled toward the couple, "Oh, this is scho-o-o beauty-ful." Wedding guests tried to catch him when he wobbled but he just brushed them away and continued his way up the aisle. Both fathers were ready to intervene but Reed waved them off. Reed marched up to Edgar and took him by the arm. "Edgar, you're drunk—"

Edgar countered, "And you're ugly, my friend. But you know what? In the morning, I'll be sober." He laughed at his own joke. No one else did.

Edgar then shook off Reed's grip, and said, "I just wanted to congratulate the bride. May I? For old times sake?"

Unwisely, Reed relented. Edgar went up to Miriam. She put out her hand but without warning Edgar grabbed her and gave her a big sloppy kiss. The guests were shocked and stood up. She pushed him away, wiping away his kiss. Reed, James, and Bailey all ran up. Reed punched Edgar to the ground. Both fathers dragged him out, the heels of his shoes leaving tracks in the lawn.

With blood trickling down his mouth Edgar promised, "I'll get you, Reed Johnson, mark my words, I'll get you."

Etta and Lethe consoled Miriam as she sat in a chair weeping. Reed came up and hugged his bride-to-be dearly. He wiped away her tears. Miriam smiled and indicated that the ceremony should continue. Such was the ominous beginning of Reed and Miriam's marriage which would reverberate throughout their relatively short and stormy relationship.

CHAPTER 4

THE AWFUL NIGHT

In the ensuing years, Reed and Miriam's vaudeville act, known as 'The Johnsons,' prospered while Edgar's, as a single performer, floundered. Edgar started taking more to drink. Once, he got on stage drunk and put on a particularly bad performance. The audience started booing him and he proceeded to harangue them. When they threw tomatoes at him, he flung his empty whiskey flask into their midst. Enough! The theater owner ordered his stage hands to forcibly pull Edgar off the stage and throw him into the back alley.

Edgar, despite being a successful solo performer before meeting Reed, could not return to that form. He sadly feared that his glory days might be over. He cursed the day he ever set eyes on Reed. "What gratitude," he thought. "I took that young whippersnapper and taught him everything I knew, and how does Reed repay him? Damn him!" By all rights, Edgar figured that he should be with Miriam, not Reed. After all, he did see her first.

With Miriam performing with Reed, Miriam's mother and father decided it was time for them to retire from the stage, settling in Baltimore in a home once owned by Etta's mother.

On the eve of the 1890s, Jimmy was born, almost literally on stage. Miriam took a few days off but soon had Jimmy in a basket off stage tended by other performers while she and Reed performed.

On the train from one town to the next, Reed was the devoted father. While Miriam held the baby, Reed would go to the dining car and cajole a bottle of warm milk from a sympathetic cook. When Miriam wanted to sleep, Reed held the baby. He loved him so much. After all, they had named him after his father.

When Jimmy was a year old, Miriam and Reed were performing in Baltimore. Miriam looked forward to this stop. She and Reed were more than happy to leave the baby with Etta and Bailey. And the doting grandparents were more than happy to spoil the child. Bailey couldn't have been prouder as he couldn't get enough of the youngster. These were Miriam's happiest days. Unfortunately, a bad heart took her dad away before he could meet his second grandson, Russell, born two years later.

When Jimmy was three, Reed saw that the boy had performing talent and started grooming him for the act, against

Miriam's better judgment. However, she could not argue with the greater success they had, now known as 'The Johnsons and Son.' The audience loved Jimmy's enthusiastic performances. At times, when Russell was sick and Miriam had to care for him, Reed and Jimmy performed as a duet.

When Russell was three, Reed saw that his second son had even a greater talent for performing than Jimmy and started grooming him to add to the act. Miriam was becoming more and more uneasy with having her sons grow up as performers. She wanted more for them, to have a life outside of the endless stream of hotel rooms, trains, and vaudeville stages.

They usually had one day off during the week. Often, Miriam would plan a picnic or a sightseeing expedition which was not much to Reed's liking. He was a workaholic who would have preferred to perfect the act.

One especially memorable trip was a foray to Coney Island when they were performing in New York. Five-year-old Jimmy could not imagine such a wonderful place. There were so many people, so many sounds, so many smells of food and the beach air. His mouth fell open when he saw the elephant-shaped hotel! He especially loved the carousel. He could ride it all day—Russell was deathly afraid of it. Miriam had to stand along side and hold Russell who closed his eyes and couldn't wait for the ride to be over. Jimmy pretended he was a cowboy, playfully taking pistol shots with his finger at his father who watched with detachment from the outside rail.

There was of course the beach and the ocean. He and Russell loved building sand castles and playing tag with the waves in their bare feet. Much later Jimmy had come to find out that the beach was segregated for coloreds. After this one day, he would not find occasion to return to Coney Island.

Reed was grumpy at the start. "A waste of time," he declared on the way to the park. He only showed a mild interest in the Civil War re-enactment of the Siege of Vicksburg. His parents had lived through that time. However, Miriam would not let him deter her or her boys of the fun she had hoped they would experience.

On the boardwalk, a man with photographic equipment asked if he could take their picture. He was a tintype photographer. A tintype was a photograph that was popular before the advent of roll film at the turn of the century. Printed on thin metal, it was more durable than glass plates, did not require a negative and was done cheaply. A tintype could be mailed or cut up for lockets. Buster Keaton played a tintype photographer in 1928 in *The Cameraman*.

Miriam readily agreed to have a photograph taken. "Come on, Reed. Let's take a picture together."

"Nah, another waste of time, and money," Reed grumbled.

She playfully sneered at him and posed by herself. Although she smiled big, Jimmy could tell that inside she was not happy. After the cameraman took her picture, she had him take a picture of the boys together. Reed could not wait to get back home.

Now the act, with three-year-old Russell joining, became known as 'The Family Johnson.' Audiences loved them. And both Jimmy and Russell enjoyed the limelight and applause. Reed and the boys wore matching outfits and derby hats. Reed always seemed to have the final word in their marriage and career but Miriam yearned for a change.

The night that Jimmy would visit in his dreams all these years started like any other night. The family finished their act and took their bows. Although it went very well, with thunderous applause from the audience, Miriam left the stage unsmiling. With the audience applauding for more, Reed brought his boys back out for another bow. He looked for Miriam but she was already in her dressing room.

Back in their hotel room, Miriam tucked the boys in for the night. She looked at them lovingly, and whispered, "Good night, Russell. Good night, J. J." She turned the gas lights off, and quietly closed the door. Russell fell right to sleep. Jimmy, tired but hyped up by the evening's performance, listened to his parents' talking in the other room. Their voices were angry. He sat up and went to the door. He cracked the door open slightly to hear them better.

The next few hours were a blur. He did remember going back to bed, then awoken in the middle of the night by his father. Reed had already packed their suitcases but why were they leaving in the middle of the night? They usually left in the morning after breakfast. Reed sternly told him to do what he said. Jimmy had to struggle to carry his own luggage filled with his and Russell's clothes. Reed carried his bag and Russell, asleep the whole time, swathed in a blanket. Still dark outside, they got on a train. But wait! Where was Mother?

At first light, the train started moving. Jimmy panicked and wanted the train to stop. He ran to the side door of the car, opened it and stuck his head out. He thought he saw a woman running after them. He muttered, "Could it be—" He heard heavy footsteps behind him and suddenly, his father sternly pulled him back in, and said, "What the hell are you doing?" Jimmy started crying and said, "Make it stop— I... I thought I saw Mother." His father quickly looked out the door but he saw no one at the rapidly receding station. He closed the door, and took a crying Jimmy back to their seat.

While his father slept on the train, Jimmy accidentally kicked open his little suitcase, spilling some clothes. As he bent down to put his clothes back in, he found the tintype of their mother taken at Coney Island. Somehow, in their haste to leave, the tintype got mixed up in his clothes. He stared at it. He never realized it before but his mother was the one person in the world that he felt closest to, and now she was suddenly and mysteriously gone. Although he couldn't articulate it, he felt a huge void that could only be filled in one way. He would have to find her and get her back. He kissed the photo and tucked it back into his suitcase.

CHAPTER 5

MIRIAM NO MORE

Baltimore, Maryland (1900). A steady drizzle fell over a cemetery. A solitary figure in dark clothing holding a black umbrella wept over a gravesite. Miriam's mother had passed away. Her father passed ten years earlier and now their graves were side by side. Having lost contact with her two sons for six years now had left her feeling especially alone and vulnerable.

Thank God she had a place to go to after that awful night when Reed took her sons away. Not only did he take the boys but he left her with the hotel bill. Damn him! But she was angrier at herself. She could have kicked herself for being so stupid. Luckily, Reed left in such a hurry that she was able to collect partial wages due from the owner of the theater where 'The Family Johnson' played last. Normally, they got paid at the end of the engagement but of course it was cut short. The money was enough to pay the hotel bill and for a one-way train ticket to Baltimore.

Her mother was a comfort and saved her life. For six months, Miriam could not leave the house. Finally, she was able to recuperate enough to look for her sons. She had guessed that Reed would still travel the vaudeville circuit that they always had. But with six months off, she didn't know where he was exactly. She traveled up and down the East Coast to the theaters they had performed in but to no avail. At the same time, she dreaded facing Reed for her indiscretion. How could she have done that? No wonder Reed did what he thought he had to do. She would too if Reed had done the same thing. But still she wanted her sons back. After six months in a futile chase, Miriam came back to Baltimore. Every week, she would check the playbills of the local vaudeville theaters but saw nothing. Eventually, she gave up looking. She guessed rightly that Reed avoided Baltimore as a stop in the Circuit.

After her mother's death, four months into the new year, as winter released its grip and buds started to bloom on trees, Miriam's spirits had begun to brighten. There was something about sunshine and springtime that fosters renewal. Miriam sat at a small table in the nearly empty house that her mother owned and left to her. A double locket on a gold chain adorned her neck. Movers were packing up the last of her mother's furniture. Soon, she would put the house up for sale with most of the furniture. She kept a few keepsake items in storage until she could retrieve them for her own home; God knows when that would be.

The previous January, the country celebrated a new year, a new decade, a new century. Not in her twenties any more, Miriam thought that it was time for her to start anew; to put all that was so hurtful behind her. She needed to look forward into this new and promising century, not backward. She told herself not to be afraid. And the first thing she wanted to do was to change her name.

On a blank sheet of paper, Miriam wrote down different names, scratching out candidates that did not suit her. Finally, she simply hit upon her middle name, Helen, and her mother's middle name, Moseley. From this day forward, she would be Helen Moseley. Miriam Johnson would be no more.

Three months later Helen found herself in New York City needing a job. She had a little money from the sale of the house but she knew that wouldn't last. She had been in vaudeville nearly all her life, but did not have the stomach to perform again. There were too many bitter memories. She was good at sewing, and found a job working on the 9th floor of a brick building with what seemed like a hundred other girls making shirtwaists. Noisy, summertime hot, working 12-hour days six days a week for $11. What was she thinking to move to this God forsaken place? Still, it put food on the table and a roof over her head.

Then she heard about a sewing job at a theater company on Broadway. She screwed up her courage and went in to see if they were still hiring. As luck would have it, they were starting a new show and desperately needed one more seamstress. After working there for awhile and recognizing her talent, the company kept her on in the costume department where she thrived. Oh, to be around theater people again. Actors and performers were people she could relate to. She began to feel alive once more. Through the ups and downs in the theater business, she worked there steadily for over ten years.

In 1911, she worked briefly for the Biograph Company, a moving picture company in town, where she met another play actor, D. W. Griffith, just getting his start as a photoplay director.

She worked in Biograph's rather modest costume department. For modern day stories, most actors had to simply bring in their own everyday clothes. She met the other actors that played in many of his flickers, including Mary Pickford, Lionel and John Barrymore, Dorothy and Lillian Gish. She and Lillian got along especially well. Helen felt a rapport with her and once while helping her with her costume for an upcoming scene, Helen tearfully broke down and told her about her two lost sons. Instead of being embarrassed or rebuking her, Gish gave her a hug and told her that she and Dorothy's own father had left the family before she could remember him. Helen appreciated the sympathy.

While the pay wasn't as good as with the theater company, Helen added to it by being an extra in crowd scenes. She found the whole process of making a moving picture fascinating. She was especially thrilled when going later into a nickelodeon to watch the moving picture she was in with an audience and a piano player accompaniment and catching glimpses of herself. In the end, though, she returned to the theater company.

Helen's personal life was mostly solitary. Once, a Negro actor in the theater company she worked for took a liking to her. Heywood Jones was an irrepressible spirit. He would not take "no" for an answer. Although she was about 40 years old, Helen was still an attractive woman. Heywood was easily five years younger. At first, Helen was flattered by his flirts and couldn't understand his attraction to her when he could have his pick of much younger women.

Finally, she gave in and they would go out to dinners after the show. She hinted at her past in vaudeville but never felt the need to reveal her marriage or her lost sons. Heywood drank heavily and tried to ply her with alcohol but she always refused. Alcohol had never agreed with her. The only beer she would drink was root beer; the only ale was ginger ale. Still it was all heady for her. She had not been in the grip of such attention since Reed. It wasn't love—she wasn't ready for that or a permanent relationship. For one thing, legally, she was still married, although she didn't have any real expectations of running into Reed again; for all practical purposes, they were divorced. And besides, Miriam Johnson was no more; she was Helen Moseley now. But still, she wasn't looking to re-marry. And neither was Heywood. However, he wanted more than just dinners and walks in the park.

Once, after dinner, while inebriated, he tried to force his physical attentions on her. She playfully resisted. He said, "Come on, Helen, what's one little kiss going to hurt?" He suddenly pinned her up against a wall and kissed her hard on the mouth. Instinctively, she pushed him away and slapped his face.

Anger filled his eyes. He growled, "Bitch. What the hell do you want?" He left, leaving Helen shaken and crying. She went home and had to examine what she did want.

Although this time she convinced herself that she didn't do anything wrong, she was filled with dread coming into work the next day. When Heywood saw her, he came over and she tensed up. He was all smiles and apologized for his behavior. She relaxed a bit and accepted his apology but she knew it would be difficult to be around him at the theater. However, something unexpected happened that day. Management had gathered all the cast and crew together to announce that ticket sales were not what they had hoped and that the show would close early. All would be out of a job. Most moaned, some cursed. Management promised to hire everyone back once they secured financing for a new show.

Helen thought about returning to the garment industry when she saw a "Now Hiring" sign at her first job in the city, for the Triangle Shirtwaist Factory. She thought about re-applying, knowing it would be only temporary work. That's when she heard about the opening at Biograph and got hired there. The following Saturday, a fire broke out at Triangle on the 8th floor. Blocked fire escapes prevented most workers in the upper floors from escaping. Some even jumped to their death rather than face the flames. All told, 146 people were killed, 129 of them young women. When Helen read the list of names of those killed, she recognized a few of them. She went to the site and saw family members looking over bodies, some charred beyond recognition, identifiable only by a necklace or shoes. She cried and said a prayer for those lost.

She realized that working for Griffith probably saved her life. She thought, "There, but for fortune." When her old theater company started work on a new show, she was re-hired. She was relieved that Heywood was not one they asked back.

Five years later, with another downturn on Broadway, her theater company folded altogether. Helen went back to Biograph to find work with Griffith. Not only was there no work, there was no Griffith. He, Gish, and company had left Biograph altogether for California. Having made hundreds of successful one- or two-reelers, that is, short films, Griffith's ambitions beckoned him to make longer pictures, four-reelers or more. That meant spending more money per film and Biograph wouldn't hear of it. He also disputed Biograph's claim that longer films would hurt audience's eyes. Since 1910, Griffith had already made a few films for Biograph in California during the harsh New England winters. By 1914, he decided to make it on his own and took his New York actors to California to start his own independent company.

Helen then heard a call for costumers at the Garden Theater putting on *Three Plays for a Negro Theater* with an all Negro cast. That would have been perfect but when she went to ask for a job, she saw Heywood milling about and she turned right around. Although it had been five years since their brief "romance," she was not anxious to revisit it. As she was reticent to face Reed since the incident, she did not relish facing Heywood. Rather than recognize this flaw in her character, she saw this instead as an opportunity to make a change. She had been in the city for over fifteen years and the winters were always brutal. A change of locale would do her good. Besides, Mr. Griffith was out there; perhaps he would have a job for her. In the least, she could put 3,000 miles between her and Heywood.

Helen closed down her life in New York, took what was left of her meager savings, and went back down to Baltimore where she sold her stored keepsake furniture and bought a one-way ticket on the transcontinental railroad to Los Angeles.

In the previous year, Griffith made a household name for himself, having made *The Birth of a Nation*, from Thomas Dixon's book, *The Clansman*. What Griffith saw as a confirmation of the stories that his Civil War Confederate colonel daddy told him as a youngster, others saw the film as horribly racist. President Wilson saw the photoplay at the White House and at first kindly called it "writing history with lightning." Upon reflection, the President would later call it an "unfortunate production." Despite the protests and controversy or perhaps because of it, *Birth* was a phenomenal financial success.

With millions of dollars in the bank, Griffith began working on an even more ambitious photoplay; one that he hoped would answer his harshest critics on *Birth*, a film to be called,

Intolerance. It was a moving picture made of four intertwining stories, each from a different era in history.

It was this project that Griffith was working on when Helen arrived in California. She took a streetcar from downtown Los Angeles to Hollywood. Tired from the long trip, she found a decent enough hotel to stay in and took in a good night sleep.

The next morning, she inquired at the front desk as to where Mr. Griffith could be found and took another streetcar to his studio at the corner of West Sunset and Hollywood Boulevards. In a residential area dotted with a few homes, Helen saw and marveled at the Babylonian set for *Intolerance* that was being constructed. Hollywood had never seen a movie set like this. Nearly a half a mile in length and taking up two city blocks, pieces were upwards of twelve stories high.

Griffith's studio was across the street from the behemoth set. Movie studio security was virtually non-existent, so Helen was able to wander onto studio grounds and found Griffith in the carpenter shop. Much was going on, noisy with a dozen carpenters sawing and hammering. They were all so busy that they didn't notice her. Griffith himself, in a suit and tie and hat, was looking at a small clay model that a craftsman brought in. It was a foot-high version of sitting up elephants that Griffith had envisioned for the set.

Griffith sketched on a piece of paper and said, "Very good. I'll need nine of these, placed so."

The craftsman looked at the sketch and said, "Twenty feet tall?"

Griffith replied, "Better make 'em thirty."

"Yes, sir. Got it, Mr. Griffith," the craftsman said as he picked up the model and the sketch and left the shop. Griffith looked up to see Helen and wracked his memory.

Walking towards him, she said, "Mr. Griffith. You probably don't remember me."

"Remind me, kind lady."

"I'm Helen Moseley, back in New York, at Biograph—"

He snapped his fingers in recognition, "Of course, Helen. You worked in costumes and in the theater district."

She extended her hand, smiled, and shook his. "Yes!"

Griffith noted, "You're mighty far from home."

"I couldn't take the winters there any longer."

Griffith chuckled and said, "As good a reason as any." He guessed what she would say next.

She looked down, paused, and then asked, "You couldn't use my help again, around here?"

Griffith looked up at a kid in his late teens in knee high pants writing notes on a clipboard, "Karl, could Sophie use any more help?"

Karl looked up, "Always, Mr. Griffith."

Griffith asked Helen, "Can you work in costumes again?"

Her face brightened, and she said, "Oh, yes!"

Griffith continued, "I have over a thousand extras that all need to be fitted for costumes."

Excited, Helen said, "I can do that, Mr. Griffith."

"Good." Griffith looked at Karl, and said, "Put Helen on the payroll. Take her to the barn."

At first excited, Helen looked concerned, and asked, "The barn?"

Griffith laughed, and said, "Don't worry—you're not going to milk cows."

Helen let out a nervous chuckle, and said, "Thank you, Mr. Griffith, thank you."

Karl walked her out of the shop towards a large building. Upstairs was a large open rehearsal stage. Underneath were the dressing rooms and sewing rooms.

Karl explained, "It's not really a barn—it's as big as one; we just call it that."

They entered. If she thought the carpenter shop was busy, activity in the barn was ten times as much. It also stored the costumes for the four stories of the picture. Besides a modern day story, Griffith was filming the story of the crucifixion of Jesus, the story of the French Huguenots in the St. Bartholomew's

Day Massacre in 1572, and, currently, the story of the fall of Babylon in 539 B.C.

Karl yelled out to a matronly woman in her forties who was in command, "Sophie."

Sophie looked up from conferring with three other dressers. Karl pointed to Helen. "More help—Helen..." He looked down on his clipboard, "Moseley."

Looking overworked, Sophie was pleased, "Good, we could use her." She waved Helen over.

Karl said, "I'll leave you in good hands," and left. Helen thanked him and went to Sophie.

Sophie asked while cutting material. "Tell me, Helen, have you worked with costumes before?"

"Oh, yes, in the theater district in New York for fifteen years and with Mr. Griffith at Biograph."

Sophie was impressed. She pointed to a row of sewing machines, and asked, "Do you know how to use one of these?"

"Yes, of course, I do."

Sophie smiled and said, "Well, you and I are going to get along just fine. Come back tomorrow morning at 8:00."

Helen asked, "Is Miss Lillian Gish around? I worked with her in New York."

"She is," Sophie said as she looked about the room. "Check dressing room number 5." Sophie pointed to the dressing rooms lined up against one wall.

Helen thanked her and went to number 5 and knocked on the door.

Gish answered from within, "Yes." Helen opened and asked, "Miss Gish. Helen Moseley." Gish was surprised but excited to see her. "Helen, my goodness, what on Earth?" The door closed as the two women reacquainted.

Thus, in the spring of 1916, Helen found herself working in Hollywood, not more than a few miles from her first born.

CHAPTER 6

NEVER ANGER POP

The first few months after the night his mother disappeared were the hardest for young Jimmy. He grieved for her as if she had died. Russell quickly got over not having Miriam around and gravitated towards Reed. Reed loved his sons and became very attentive to them. But when he had to struggle with chores that Miriam used to do, like feeding the family and washing clothes, he would curse her. In Reed's mind, they had a good thing going, and she ruined it. Damn her. Damn her to Hell!

Eventually, Jimmy gave in to his new reality. Their act, now known as 'Johnson and Sons,' was very successful. Jimmy couldn't deny that Reed steered their professional development brilliantly. As they got older, while Russell came around to fully embrace being on stage, Jimmy was beginning to lose his ardor for it. He enjoyed being with his brother and for now that would be enough. But Reed was a hard taskmaster that Jimmy frequently crossed.

Between shows, Jimmy found a fascination with gadgets and machinery. Jimmy loved taking things apart and putting them back together. He carried a small tool kit with him wherever they went. At the turn of the twentieth century, inventions abounded. Thomas Edison himself was credited with over a thousand patents. It was a world of wonder. Cities and homes were getting electricity, telephones, and automobiles. Office buildings were getting taller and taller and had elevators. Household drudgery became less so with washing machines, ice boxes, and other labor saving kitchen devices. Automobiles fascinated Jimmy to no end. He dreamed of owning one and being able to fix it.

Also between shows, Jimmy tried to get his father to teach him and Russell how to read and write. It was something Jimmy thought his mother would have wanted. Reading stories to him and Russell was something his mother did after performances. Since Reed had only a rudimentary knowledge and was embarrassed by his lack of proper schooling, he would push away Jimmy's request. Miriam was an avid reader and she had handled all the written agreements the act entered into. By the time Miriam was gone, Reed knew all the vaudeville promoters and vaudeville house owners pretty well and a gentleman's agreement, a handshake, and an "X" on a contract would seal the deal. Still, Reed recognized that someone in the family should be able to read and write and Jimmy seemed most eager. Reed enlisted the help of other vaudevillians, mostly other women performers, who took a motherly interest in the formal education of the two young boys. As his mother, Jimmy became an avid reader.

Reed reluctantly realized that the boys needed time off even if he didn't. So, on their days off, he would take them to a park, a carnival, a beach. The boys would throw a ball around or just run. Jimmy knew how to make kites and he and Russell would have a grand time having "dogfights," trying to knock each other's kite out of the sky. Jimmy loved having his brother around. He couldn't imagine what life would be like if he was alone with Reed.

Chicago, Illinois (1909). 'Johnson and Sons' was playing a theater owned and managed by Sam Bixby, a Negro man in his mid-forties. Sam worked in the theater business most of his life, never as a performer but he had a talent for recognizing talent. He had met Reed and his sons shortly after Miriam disappeared. Sam had been working as a backstage crew member, and he became good friends with Reed and watched the boys grow up and develop. Reed never talked about the boys' mother and Sam didn't pry.

Jimmy got more and more tired of performing. He wanted to do something else with his life but he could never get up the nerve to tell his father. Each performance took a little more out of him. It was torture—death from a thousand cuts. It started to show up in his work which made Reed angrier at him. This made Jimmy more frustrated and alienated. It was a vicious cycle and unfortunately there was only one way to break it.

For publicity, Reed hired a photographer to take a couple of pictures of him and his two boys in their coordinated suits and derby hats. It happened at an evening performance that Jimmy wished was over. In the pose, Reed smiled as did Russell. Jimmy did not. Flash!

The photographer looked at Jimmy and said, "Smile, sonny."

Jimmy forced a smile. And flash a second time. Done.

Reed asked, "When will the pictures be ready?"

"Give me two days."

"You got it."

Sam walked up to Reed with another man dressed in a business suit and said, "Reed, and boys, I've got a train to catch."

Reed and Russell looked at Sam. Jimmy had his back turned, a million miles away, biting on his fingernails.

Reed said to Sam, "What's this crap about you leaving town?"

"I'm opening a theater in California."

"California? There's nothing out there."

"Nothing but opportunity. I've been there—you'd be surprised." Sam slaps the man next to him on the back. "My brother, Howard, here will take care of you."

A stagehand watching the act on stage called out "'Johnson and Sons,' you're on in five."

Sam said, "All right, I've gotta run. Listen, if you ever get out to the West Coast—"

Reed shook Sam's hand. Now, to his sons, "Come on, boys, one more show tonight."

Jimmy was still deep in thought. Reed went to him and snapped his fingers in his face. He said, "Jimmy. Jimmy." Jimmy looked blankly at his dad who said, "Where are you, boy? We're on."

Russell was eager while Jimmy sighed with trepidation. He just couldn't do this anymore and dragged himself behind his brother. He took a deep breath as they waited their turn. On stage, two performers were performing their last bit. Both held prop telephones.

"Hello, law firm of Douglas, Douglas, Douglas, and Douglas."

"Yes, let me speak to Mr. Douglas."

"He's dead these six years. We keep his name on the door out of respect."

"Then let me speak to Mr. Douglas."

"He's on vacation."

Exasperated, "Well then, let me speak to Mr. Douglas!"

"He's out to lunch."

Yelling, "Then let me speak to Mr. Douglas!!"

"Speaking."

There was only a smattering of appreciation. The performers looked at each other surprised. This usually got the biggest laugh. The performers bowed, got off, and passed the Johnsons.

"Good luck, Reed. The asbestos is down."

Reed thanked him. "Hear that, boys? Gotta work extra hard. Let's give 'em a bang-up job." He and his sons ran on and got into their opening positions. The piano player started playing.

Jimmy could not focus on his performance. In the middle of the act, he made a wrong turn and bumped into Russell. The crowd snickered. Reed seethed as he danced next to Jimmy. Under his breath, he told him, "Get with it. You're embarrassing us."

That did it. Jimmy stopped, stared at Reed who was still tap dancing about. Reed tried not to get distracted until

Jimmy tossed down his cane and walked off the stage. The crowd murmured, wondering if this was part of the act.

Russell stopped, as did Reed. Reed tapped Russell on a shoulder and indicated how they should exit the stage, side-stepping with their canes pushing in and out. Russell hastily picked up Jimmy's cane. The piano player was perplexed but played exit music to confused applause.

The hotel room that the Johnsons were staying in had a living room with a sofa, a chair, a floor lamp, and a folded up roll away bed. To one side there was a small dining table with three chairs. A bedroom adjoined, wash room down the hall. Tension filled the air as the three Johnsons made their way to their room. Reed, fuming, fumbled while getting the door unlocked which angered him more. After his sons entered, he slammed close the door. Reed raged at Jimmy, "What the hell was that about?"

"Pop. I'm sorry but I just can't do this anymore."

"Do what?"

"I... I have to quit the act."

Russell was stunned and Reed couldn't believe what he was hearing. "What are you talking about? Hear that, Russell?

He wants to quit the act." Now, to Jimmy, "After all I've done for you..."

Jimmy said, "It's not that I'm ungrateful but it's not what I want to do with the rest of my life. I'm twenty—"

"And, so, what do want to do? Be a bum?" Loudly, to an imaginary audience, Reed announced, "Yes, folks. This is my son, the bum. Throw a penny into his cup!"

Jimmy tried to hold his ground, "I can get a job. I'm good with my hands. I can fix things."

Reed scoffed, "Fix things? I saw what you did to my watch. I had to pay good money to get it fixed proper."

Russell tried to help his brother, "He was only ten—"

"Shut up! You're not taking his side."

Reed was done arguing. "Okay, smart guy."

Reed went to a closet and took out Jimmy's suitcase. He threw it on the bed and flung it open. He went into the boy's bedroom and returned with some of Jimmy's clothes which he tossed into the suitcase.

Anxiously, Jimmy asked, "What are you doing?"

Reed went back into the bedroom and returned with more of Jimmy's clothes, and tossed them into the suitcase. "You want to leave? Then, leave!! You're just like your moth—" He stopped himself.

"What? Just like our mother?" Feeling emboldened, he asked, "What did happen to our mother!?"

This infuriated Reed more. He snapped shut the suitcase and opened the front door. Russell tried to intervene. "Pop, no!"

"Get out of my way!" Reed pushed Russell aside and tossed the suitcase into the hall.

Jimmy realized what he had to do. He ran into the bedroom and lifted the mattress of his bed. He took out a sock and opened it to reveal cash. Also in the sock was the tintype photograph of his mother taken at Coney Island. He stuffed the cash and tintype back into the sock, the sock into his pocket.

Jimmy went back into the living room. From the front closet, he hastily grabbed his overcoat, flinging the coat hanger onto the floor. Russell was in anguish.

"Bye, Russell. I'm sorry. I didn't want it to end this way."

Russell told Jimmy, "Wait!" He ran into the bedroom and quickly returned with cash, giving it to Jimmy. Jimmy took it and hugged his brother.

With tears in his eyes, Jimmy said, "I'll pay you back. Promise. I'll pay you back."

Jimmy looked at his father and said, "Bye, Pop."

Reed only grunted. Jimmy walked out the door. Reed slammed it behind him. Only now did Reed start to calm down. "I say, good riddance." He tried to comfort Russell,

"You've always had the talent in the family." Russell couldn't think. Wiping away tears, he marched into the bedroom, slamming the door.

Reed said loudly through the bedroom door, "I've got some great ideas for a two-man act, like from the old days."

Reed sat down on the sofa. He looked back at the bedroom door. He didn't allow himself to think of what had just happened. Softly, to himself, he said, "Russell doesn't think it now but he'll see. We'll be better than ever." Nodding his head, he reaffirmed, "Yes, better than ever."

Out in the hotel hall, Jimmy picked up his suitcase. He looked back one last time, and wiped away a final tear. He was resolute. He would cry no more about this. He went down the stairs, unsure of what his future would hold, not knowing when—or even if—he would see them again.

CHAPTER 7

WINTERBOUND

L ife without his father and brother was difficult and scary for Jimmy. What did he know about living – living living on his own? He stayed in a cheap hotel and ate very little, fearful of running out of the money that he had.

He went down to the theater where 'Johnson and Sons' was playing and saw that their act was crossed out on the bill. He sought out Sam, knocking on his office door.

A different voice answered, "Come in."

Jimmy opened the door and saw Howard behind Sam's desk. "Howard? Is Sam around?"

"No, didn't you hear? He's in California—"

"California!?"

"I thought he told you. Anyway, I've taken over here. Can I help you?"

"Are my dad and Russell still here?"

"No, they up and left. Poof, just like that." Howard laughed, "What happened? Did they forget to tell you?"

"Actually, I quit the act."

Howard's eyes widened as he leaned back in his captain's chair. "Really? Reed never mentioned."

"Did they go on to Detroit?"

"I believe so. I don't know why. Reed came into the office yesterday, saying they had to leave and could they get paid? I reminded him that they did have another week but he had a burr under his saddle. Say, are you planning a solo career?" Howard looked at his schedule book. "If so, I do have a spot available."

"Thanks, Howard, but I'm getting out of the business altogether."

Howard stopped looking at his book and sat back in his chair. "Well, good luck, son. If you change your mind, see me." Howard stood up and shook Jimmy's hand.

Jimmy smiled, turned, and left the office. As he cut through the back stage where stagehands were preparing for that evening's shows, Jimmy looked at what had been his home, his life, his anchor for all of his years. The look, the sounds, the smells, the people. For all that irked him about the business and his dad, there was a familiarity and comfort about the theater that he couldn't deny. He took a deep breath. He felt as if he was stepping off a cliff and wondered where he would land.

He guessed that his dad and Russell were headed east towards New York and then down the eastern seaboard. He thought about chasing them down but what was the point? He wanted to leave the act and now he had. Besides, his dad threw him out. He would feel foolish trying to return. What could he say, that he made a frickin' mistake? Reed could carry a grudge and he would never let Jimmy forget it. No, no, Jimmy couldn't take that.

That night, lying in bed trying to fall asleep, listening to a couple arguing in the next room, Jimmy wondered if this was how his mother felt after that terrible night fifteen years before. During those fifteen years, he had felt a whole range of emotions about his mother, from unconditional love to confusion to betrayal. Now he felt empathy. Now, more than ever, he needed to find her and ask her, "Why? What happened?"

"Baltimore," he thought. "Wasn't that where his mother's parents lived?" He was only a year old at the time but he had been told that he had met his grandfather before he died. Of course, he couldn't remember the house but what were their names? Etta and Bailey... what? While wracking his brain, he fell asleep.

Waking up the next morning, their last name popped in his head. The vaudeville act his mother was in was called 'The Hopkins Trio.' Bailey and Etta Hopkins. He counted his money, checked out of the hotel, and bought a one-way train ticket to Baltimore. He promised himself that once he gave up life on the road, that he would never take the train again. He associated the train with his mother's disappearance and the agonizing days in vaudeville. But the thought of going from Chicago to Baltimore by hitching a ride in the back of a truck at the start of winter had even less appeal. There weren't very many trucks around and who would stop to pick up a colored man for such a long trip?

What should have been a two day train ride stretched to five days, thanks to weather delays and a bridge washout. By the time he got to Baltimore, he couldn't wait to get off the steam belching monster.

It took him another three days but he did track down his grandparents' house. Unfortunately, the people living there weren't his grandparents, or his mother. The family had bought the house from a Miriam Johnson nine years before, and no, they did not know where she went. He thanked them for their time.

Jimmy was able to find his grandparents' gravesite. He imagined his mother standing in the very same spot. In the snow and bitter cold, he mourned for them and for himself. California. He heard of sunshine year round there from the vaudeville acts that ventured out to the West Coast. Yes, he decided that he too would find his destiny in California.

Of course, it was the dead of winter now. He would have to suffer another train ride out west. At the train station, he only had enough money to get to Denver. That would have to do. In the spring, he could finish the trip to California. That meant getting a job in Denver right away. But, hell, didn't he boast to his father that he could do that? As he sat down in the coach, he thought of that old adage, "Be careful what you wish for."

The train ride to Denver was uneventful, thank God. But, getting in after dark and standing on the train platform in the mile high city, man, it was cold. He ran inside the station and asked for directions for a place to stay. He was directed from downtown, to what he guessed was a destitute part of town. That didn't matter—all he needed was a room with heat.

At his boarding room, he turned on the steam radiator which clanked and sputtered. "Oh, no," he thought. But then he felt the heat coming on. He rubbed his hands together over it to thaw them out. He had a pair of gloves but darn unfortunate that both he and his dad neglected to pack them when Reed threw him out. He also forgot his handy little tool kit. Damn. There were tools in there he had since he was ten. Once he got a job, he would put together a new one. He then plopped himself down on the bed with his hands pushed under his armpits and fell promptly to sleep. He didn't awake until noon the next day, still in his clothes and overcoat.

Miracle of miracles, the room was warm and the sun was out. He looked out the window. The glistening snow was in a way beautiful. That didn't make looking for work any less bearable, not when you could see your breath as you trudged through the drifts. Towards the evening, after many "no thank yous," slammed doors, and turned over "Help Wanted" signs, Jimmy came across an automobile garage. The owner, John McCormick, was struggling to move a 55 gallon oil drum. Jimmy ran in and helped him.

McCormick indicated a back corner of the garage, and said, "Over there."

Both men got their hands dirty. McCormick grabbed two rags and tossed one to Jimmy who wiped off his hands. He thanked Jimmy.

Jimmy asked, "You wouldn't be looking for some help here?"

McCormick sized him up and said, "Have you worked in a garage before, around automobiles?"

"No, but the first time I saw a car on the road, I promised myself that I was going to own one." McCormick looked down. Jimmy continued, "I love machinery, taking things apart and fixing them. When I was a kid, I once took apart my father's pocket watch."

McCormick asked, "How did that go?"

Jimmy chuckled, "I got most of the parts back." McCormick smiled. Jimmy continued, "I can sweep, clean. I want to learn everything there is to know about fixing cars."

"Well, I could use some help in emptying oil drums, maybe changing tires. Denver's getting more and more automobiles, and I can barely keep up with the work. I tried a couple of kids from the high school but they couldn't piss on the ground and make it foam." Jimmy hoped he wouldn't have to demonstrate. McCormick then said, "I can't pay much."

"Whatever you think is fair."

McCormick held out his hand, "All right—what's your name?"

Jimmy shook his hand, and said, "Jimmy Johnson."

"John McCormick. I expect you to be in at 7 a.m. every morning, Monday through Saturday. I don't take to slackers."

Jimmy was jubilant, and said, "Thank you. Thank you. You won't be sorry. I'll be here 7 a.m. sharp."

McCormick watched Jimmy leave. He then turned off the light, closed the big double doors of his garage and locked it. He wondered if he didn't just make a huge mistake.

For the first time since Chicago, Jimmy ate a decent hot meal.

Unsure about hiring a black man, McCormick, in the first few days, kept a close eye on Jimmy. Jimmy was aware of this and wasn't about to do anything that would get him fired.

This was a dream job for Jimmy. He got to work around machines and tools, tools he never used or even heard about. At first he did menial chores, like keeping the garage clean, shoveling snow, and dumping old oil into drums that would be dumped into a pit in the back come spring thaw. McCormick even taught him how to fix flat tires.

Eventually, McCormick relaxed about Jimmy. He saw what future employers would see—that Jimmy had skills, was a quick learner, and was dependable. Eventually, McCormick started to teach Jimmy about cars. Jimmy learned how to change a carburetor and tune an engine. He even helped McCormick rebuild an engine. With the engine apart, McCormick was able to explain to Jimmy how the internal combustion engine worked, an absolute marvel of engineering. It was a real eye opener for Jimmy.

With the spring thaw, a big lump of snow in the back melted away, revealing an abandoned car. All four tires were flat, the body had started to rust, the fabric top was torn, the front bumper was missing, and there was a big dent in the radiator. Jimmy asked McCormick about it, "Say, boss, what's going on with that car?"

"Oh, a farmer in these parts, Ollie Winslow, drove it in last year. He had hit a tree—couldn't get the hang of driving it—and sold it to me for pennies on the dollar. He said that a horse and wagon had served him well in all his born days and it would again. I haven't had time to deal with it. I was actually going to sell it for scrap or use it for parts."

Jimmy's eyes lit up. "Could I buy it from you? You can take it out of my wages."

"What do you want with it?"

"I'm going to fix it. And learn to drive."

McCormick chuckled, "Are you sure? It needs a lot of work. But, okay."

During the spring and early summer, Jimmy was all over that car like flies on honey. It was a labor of love. Jimmy worked on it at night, weekends, during slow times at the garage. The engine was still good. Radiator and bumper had to be replaced. And four new tires. At last the big day came. Crossing their fingers for luck, McCormick put gasoline in the tank and tried to start the car with the crank in the front.

He instructed Jimmy on the dangers of the hand crank. He said, "Be sure to cup your hand under the crank and pull up. The natural tendency is to wrap your whole hand around it. If the engine backfires, it could break your thumb. Doc Martin has fixed many a broken wrist around here because of it." McCormick demonstrated. One turn, nothing. Jimmy was worried. McCormick poured a little gasoline down the throat of the carburetor. A second turn, a sputter. A mighty third turn and the engine kicked over. Jimmy jumped for joy as he heard the engine running. Idling rough, sure, but it was running! McCormick turned it off. He told Jimmy, "Now, you start it. Cup it. Good." Jimmy smiled as he got it started on the first try. Jimmy spent the whole of the next day off tuning it up.

After much pestering, McCormick taught Jimmy how to drive. With open roads and only a few cars about, Jimmy had plenty of opportunities to make mistakes, like grinding the gears while shifting. This gave McCormick heartburn.

"Dammit, Jimmy," he said. "You strip those gears and the car ain't going nowhere for a long time." This outburst reminded Jimmy of his father but for McCormick's patience, Jimmy finally got the hang of it and became a good driver. McCormick was proud of his work but he vowed never to teach anyone again.

It was the start of summer and Jimmy still hadn't forgotten about California. As much as he loved working at the garage, he knew that if he didn't leave soon, he would have to endure another Denver winter. McCormick was sorry to see Jimmy go but understood. He gave Jimmy a few extra tools for his tool kit and an extra spare tire. Before he left, Jimmy was sure to get a driver's license and a car registration. The last thing he wanted to be in the middle of nowhere spending some time in county jail on a false car theft charge.

With a little money saved up, Jimmy thanked McCormick and with a handshake, he got into his car. Oops, Jimmy almost forgot. He opened a small paper bag and took out a brand new tweed driver cap and proudly put it on. McCormick had to smile. Jimmy honked once and started driving west full of hope. All McCormick prayed for was that the car would make it up the eastern slopes of the High Sierras.

CHAPTER 8

GO WEST YOUNG MAN

Jimmy was all smiles as he drove through town. Gawkers stared in wonder at who was driving. One asked, "Say, isn't that Ollie Winslow's old car?" Jimmy honked his horn more than once to those who pointed. No matter as Jimmy said "good-bye" to Denver once and for all.

Once out of town, Jimmy took the dusty and unpaved roads that served oxen and covered wagons years before, going from Denver, through Salt Lake City, up the Sierras to Reno, down to Sacramento, then to San Francisco. He needed to get over the Sierras before the snows came. He thought he could. After all, it was only late June.

For the most part he slept in his car, buying food along the way. He had no trouble with the car except for a couple of flat tires. Once, in the hot afternoon sun near the Bonneville Salt Flats, the car overheated. One thing he forgot to do was to refill his water pouch. Stupid!

A couple of cars drove past but didn't stop. Jimmy cursed them. Then a deputy sheriff drove up. Twice already in Wyoming, he was stopped by local constables who were more than suspicious of a black man driving a car. With his proper papers, they begrudgingly let him proceed.

With his hood up, Jimmy approached the deputy who had stepped out of his car. Jimmy said, "Thank God, you showed up—"

The deputy pulled out his revolver and pointed it at Jimmy. "What are you doing with that automobile?"

Jimmy's mouth dropped. "I own it—"

"Shut up! What kind of fool do you take me for?"

"I got registration papers—" said Jimmy as he turned to get the papers out of the car.

"Hold it right there." Jimmy stopped. "Hands up. NOW!"

Jimmy shot his hands skyward and indicated inside, "Go see for yourself. In the glove box."

Holding the gun on Jimmy, the deputy found the papers. "I'm going to have to take you back to the station and check this out."

"Just look at the papers—"

"Oh, resisting an arrest."

"What!"

The deputy handcuffed Jimmy and pushed him into the back seat of the police car. Jimmy thought, "This is not happening."

At the station, the deputy put Jimmy in a cell by himself. Other cells had other prisoners. The deputy put the cell keys on a hook near his desk and tossed Jimmy's papers into a desk drawer. Jimmy protested, "Hey, aren't you going to check out the papers?"

"Shit for brains. I need to call Colorado authorities and they be closed by now. The Sheriff will have to do it in the morning."

"My car overheated! You can't put me in jail for that. Get me out of here, you bast—"

Angered, the deputy got up into Jimmy's face while waving a billy club, and said, "Keep yapping like that, boy, and you'll be in there for a long, long time."

Jimmy cringed at the word, "boy." Knowing that other bogus charges could be trumped up, Jimmy held his tongue for the rest of the night. He lay down on the cot with creaky springs.

Late that night, listening to coyotes in the distant hills baying at the nearly full moon, Jimmy couldn't help but stew. No white man would be jailed for simply driving a car. It brought back all the memories of the racist shit he, Russell, and his father had to endure during their vaudeville travels, from the flea bitten, rat infested hotels, to the health department condemned restaurants, to separate toilet facilities, to having to use back entrances instead of the front. And that was traveling in the North. In the Deep South, he heard about the lynchings that the local law would do nothing about. His father just took it, saying that that was just the way it was. But, why? Why did it have to be that way? Why couldn't black people be treated with respect, too? One day, attitudes would have to change.

The next morning, Jimmy was awakened by his iron cell door clanking open. The Sheriff, a heavy set man in his sixties with a handlebar moustache, held the keys and the open door. Looking at Jimmy's driver's license, he said, "James Reed Johnson, you are free to go."

He gave Jimmy back his papers and said, "Sorry. Deputy Crowley was a might overcautious." He indicated another deputy sheriff. "Deputy Smith here will take you back to your car with a bucket of water."

Back at his car, after filling the radiator with water, Jimmy started the car. The deputy left him with a canvas pouch filled with water and said, "Not a good idea to travel in the desert without extra water." Jimmy thanked him and they parted ways, Jimmy west, the deputy back east. Jimmy couldn't wait to get to California.

When Jimmy rolled into Reno, Nevada on July 4, 1910, he was shocked. What he had heard would be a sleepy town was as bustling as Chicago. He then saw a poster for the "Fight of the Century." Jack Johnson, a black man, was to fight James Jeffries, a white boxer, for the heavyweight champion title. Johnson was already the heavyweight champion, having defeated Tommy Burns in Australia the year before. Author Jack London called for "A Great White Hope" to take away the title from Johnson. Jeffries, a former heavyweight champion, came out of retirement to be that hope.

Jimmy had originally planned on moving onto California right away but decided to stay to watch the fight if possible. About 20,000 people crowded into the fight arena in downtown Reno. Jimmy stood outside the gates with all the others who didn't have tickets.

One thing that Jimmy saw was men carrying in huge motion picture cameras from several motion picture company trucks. One truck mentioned "Hollywood, California" on the side. This fight was to be filmed. Jimmy had an idea. Many workers were hauling in movie equipment. He got in line and grabbed two canisters of film. A foreman caught him. "Hey, you!" Jimmy froze.

The foreman just pointed to a man carrying a tripod. "Follow that guy."

Jimmy smiled, "Yes, sir." When he got into the arena, he saw several movie cameras being set up—many companies were filming this fight from different angles. The guy with the tripod yelled out, "Stan Crawford!"

A cameraman up on a platform raised his hand, and said, "Here!" The guy with the tripod and Jimmy climbed up onto the platform with a good view of the ring. Stan set his camera up on the tripod and fastened it. The guy who brought up the tripod went back down and Stan turned to Jimmy holding the film canisters. He took a good look at Jimmy, and asked, "Who are you?"

"Jimmy." Jimmy shrugged and smiled, "I wanted to see the fight."

Stan smiled and chuckled, "You got chutzpah, kid. Stay close, and hand me one of those canisters."

Jimmy did so and watched how Stan threaded the film in the camera.

After much delay, the fight got started. Jimmy not only saw one of the greatest boxing matches in history but he also saw how cameramen were filming the fight, looking through a lens and hand cranking the camera. Jimmy wondered if their arms ever got tired. Part way through the fight, Stan had to quickly change film during a break between rounds. When the fight was over with Johnson's victory over Jeffries, to the great disappointment of the predominately white crowd, Stan warned Jimmy, "Kid, you better scoot out of here, pronto. This crowd is none too happy."

"Thanks." Jimmy did not argue and scurried out. The cameraman was right—the crowd was in no mood to be kind to people of color. In fact, that night, amid fireworks that celebrated the birth of a nation that proclaimed that all men were created equal, it was with great irony that so many race riots in cities across the country took place as whites vented their frustration. There seemed to be no hope in finding a "Great White Hope." Three days after the event, many cities and states banned the showing of the fight film.

The next day, on the 5th, trainload after trainload took journalists and disappointed fight fans east and west, returning Reno to the quiet town that Jimmy had imagined it would be. Something about the motion picture cameras caught Jimmy's attention, and he attended his first picture show that night. He and Russell never had a chance to see a movie while traveling with their dad. His dad didn't care for it. "Here today, gone tomorrow," he predicted. What Jimmy saw on the screen that night was beyond belief. This was pure magic. He stayed to watch a second show.

The next day he got into his car and started to challenge the Sierras. He took it slow at first, not wanting to tax his car. McCormick warned him that this would be the most grueling part of the journey. Horse drawn and diesel lumber trucks carrying newly cut trees to saw mills passed him coming down into Nevada. Before he reached the crest, his car started to overheat again. "Shit," he cursed. He couldn't risk stopping— he might not get it started again. If he can just get over the crest, it would be downhill to Sacramento. He had to push it. But the car wouldn't take it. It had given its all. Jimmy heard a gut-wrenching "pop" from under the hood and the engine froze. He pulled over and stopped, setting the parking brake. He got out and his loud cussing echoed through the hills. He kicked a tire in frustration, stubbing a toe. Opening the hood, steam spewed into the air from the radiator. Maybe all that he needed to do was to add more water to the radiator. He did have bags of water this time. But he would have to wait until the engine cooled down. McCormick warned him not to add water while the engine was hot—he could crack the engine block.

After a few hours, no more steam, so Jimmy opened the radiator cap, and added water. Crossing his fingers, he turned on the ignition and tried the crank. It would not budge. "Dammit all to hell! Infernal combustion engine!!"

Almost there, he was at a crossroads. He could walk or hitch a ride back to Reno, get a tow wagon but he would most likely have to spend the winter there, or he could abandon his car, walk or hitch a ride to Sacramento, and take a train from there to San Francisco. He decided that the first person who could give him a ride in either direction would decide his fate.

During the rest of the day, no one would stop. He spent a freezing night in the car. The next morning, hoping against hope, he said a little prayer, and tried to crank the car over. It still wouldn't budge. Just as he was about to cuss some more, an empty diesel lumber truck came up from the east. The driver took pity and stopped.

The driver said, "Got trouble, huh?"

Jimmy looked exasperated, "The engine froze on me. Can you give me a tow?"

"How's your brakes?"

"Fine, as far as I can tell."

"I'm headed to Sacramento but I can tow you to a garage in Truckee."

"You're a life saver, mister."

The driver got out of his truck, grabbed a heavy rope, tied it to the back of his truck and tossed the other end to Jimmy who fastened it to the front frame of his car.

The driver said, "On down hills, work the brake. Honk if you need for me to stop."

"Got it."

The driver got into his truck and started it as Jimmy got into his car. Jimmy put his foot on the brake and released the emergency brake. The truck started slowly up the first hill to tighten the rope. Jimmy slowly released his foot from the brake and his car started gingerly up the grade with the truck.

Getting pulled uphill was easy but when they went downhill, Jimmy had to learn quickly to squeeze the brake so as to not run into the back of the truck or snap the rope. It was hard going the whole time. Jimmy silently rejoiced when he saw the sign marking the border between Nevada and California. He thought, "It shouldn't be long now."

After a few more trips up and down hills, the driver sounded his horn and pointed. Jimmy saw Truckee in the distance and started to feel relief.

When they got into town, the truck stopped at a service station and dropped Jimmy and his car off. Jimmy thanked the man while helping him untie his rope. Jimmy promised himself to help others when he could. The truck stopped at a restaurant across the street and the driver went in. Jimmy found the owner of the garage, a short man in a greasy overall. He had red hair and a bushy red beard.

"Hi."

"Hello."

"The engine died. Can you fix it?"

"Let's take a look."

The smallish but muscular owner tried to start it with a hefty effort but, as Jimmy found, the crank wouldn't budge.

The owner said, "Whew. Might have blown a piston. Won't know 'til we take her apart."

"Well, how long will that take?"

The owner pulled on his beard in thought and said, "I reckon it could be a couple of months."

"What!?"

The owner pointed to a number of disabled vehicles on his lot, and said, "Got these others to do first. After we find out what's wrong with your car, we got to order parts from back east—"

"Okay, okay." An exasperated Jimmy looked up at the darkening sky. First, he really didn't have the money for such a major repair unless he got a job. And, if he waited too long and the snows came, he'll be stuck again for another winter. Jimmy asked, "What would you take for it? It's got a new carburetor and new tires."

The owner rocked on his heels, and bargained, "I'll give you fifty bucks."

"Sixty?"

"Fifty-five's the best I can do." While he certainly spent more than that to get the car in good working order, Jimmy didn't have much choice. "All right."

The owner and Jimmy shook hands. Jimmy signed over the papers and the owner gave Jimmy the cash. Just then, Jimmy saw the benevolent truck driver come out of the restaurant. He had a toothpick in his mouth and started to get into his truck. Jimmy grabbed his tools, suitcase, and overcoat out of his car. He ran over and asked the truck driver for a ride to Sacramento.

The truck driver said "okay" but Jimmy would have to ride in the back of the truck. That would be fine with him. Jimmy got on and leaned up against the back wall. He banged on the cab to let the driver know he was ready. As the truck pulled away, he watched with sadness as his first car faded into the distance.

CHAPTER 9

IN THE LAND OF DREAMS

A few hours later, Jimmy woke up from a nap and saw the distant Sierras. The truck slowed down and stopped at a train station. They had arrived in Sacramento. The driver stuck his head out of his window, and said, "This is your stop, pal." Jimmy grabbed his gear and thanked the man kindly once again. He decided to stay one night in town before heading out.

Lying in bed at yet another flea-bitten hotel, Jimmy kept thinking about the movies and movie cameras. How did they work their magic? The next day, he went to a pawn shop and bought a small movie camera. Because he still had his tools, he was able to take the camera apart and put it back together. A wondrous machine.

He bought a train ticket for San Francisco, arriving there a week after Reno. It was reported that Mark Twain had said that the coldest winter he ever spent was a summer in San Francisco.

The fog, the area's natural air conditioning, was particularly overbearing that year. Jimmy couldn't believe that he had to wear his overcoat during the day in July! He needed to get to warmer weather. Folks told him that Los Angeles was always sunny and warm. Hollywood was there, too, where those movie trucks in Reno came from. This struck a chord with Jimmy.

Because he had only a few dollars left, Jimmy sold his tools, pawned the movie camera, and bought yet another train ticket to what people called the land of dreams. He took the ferry across the bay to Oakland, and then boarded the Southern Pacific to downtown Los Angeles.

When he arrived, he spent a miserable night in yet another broken down hotel. The next morning, he asked how to get to Hollywood. He was told that a streetcar was available but he was tired of trains and vowed never to take one again. He walked and hitched a ride to Sunset Boulevard, stopping across the street from the Sunset Camera Shop. It had a "Help Wanted" sign in the window. As Louis Pasteur once said, "Chance favors the prepared mind."

He went in to inquire about the job. The owner, Andrew Callahan, opened Sunset Camera in 1905 shortly after Hollywood incorporated. Callahan, in his late 40s, was an Irishman with a thick moustache. In the 1880s, Callahan's father had been a rather successful landscape photographer, often taking his young son trudging through the wilderness of the West with large wet plate camera equipment. While Andrew shared his father's passion for photography, he did not share his father's tolerance for the hardship of photographing in the outdoors. He decided to open a shop.

When the store first opened, Callahan sold large wet plate photographic equipment but soon got into the more popular box cameras, folding cameras, stereoscopic cameras and viewers. With a full line of the new easy-to-use Kodak cameras, Callahan started a developing and printing film service. Then, in 1910, the first movie studios started to open up in town. Callahan, recognizing the trend, started selling moving picture cameras, projectors, and movie film stock.

Callahan was in the back room helping an employee with a broken camera when a store clerk brought in Jimmy. The three workers sitting at benches fixing cameras looked up.

The clerk said, "Boss, someone here who wants the job."

Callahan looked up, saw Jimmy, and frowned. No other employees in his store were people of color. He picked up a rag and wiped off his hands and went to Jimmy. Callahan said, "Sorry, boy, but we're looking for someone who can repair cameras."

Jimmy thought, "There was that word again." And again this was no time to get agitated by it.

"Cameras? I can do that, and I'm a quick learner."

"We ain't a school. Do you have any experience?"

"I worked in an automobile repair garage in Denver for eight months. I built my own car and drove it out until it broke down in Truckee."

Callahan wasn't convinced. "Cameras ain't cars."

"But they both have moving parts."

"Sorry but—"

"I really need this job—I can work for free this week, and if you aren't convinced that I can be a valuable employee, we can part ways."

Callahan mulled this over, "No camera work, though."

"I worked with a cameraman, Stan Crawford..."

Callahan's face perked up and said, "I know Crawford. Here in Hollywood?"

"No, in Reno, at the big fight there."

Callahan got excited. "You mean, Johnson and Jeffries? You were there?"

Jimmy nodded, and said, "I got to see it, and helped Stan film it." Callahan whistled, and said, "I saw that footage before they pulled it." This also piqued the interest of the other workers who for the first time stopped what they were doing and took a good look at Jimmy.

Jimmy continued, "I also owned an Ernemann Kino once. Took it apart, and put it back together."

Callahan walked over to a shelf cluttered with discarded cameras, rummaged through it, and pulled one out. He tossed it to Jimmy, and said, "Like this one?"

Jimmy held a camera similar to one he bought in Sacramento. "Yes, very much like this one."

Callahan pointed to an empty bench. "Let's see you take it apart and put it back together."

Jimmy sighed, and sat down. He looked around, and asked, "Some tools?"

Callahan looked at one of his employees, and beckoned, "Ferguson, some tools." Ferguson begrudgingly brought over a handful of tools. Jimmy got to work. It didn't take long for Callahan to see that Jimmy was adept and had skills.

Callahan said, "All right. Very good. What's your name?"

"Jimmy Johnson."

"I'm Callahan. All right, Jimmy. Come back tomorrow morning at 8 a.m. Let's see what you can do in a week."

After that first week, Callahan liked what he saw in Jimmy's work. He hired him and paid him for the "free" week. With earned money once again in his pockets, Jimmy was able to get a decent apartment. No more rat-infested boarding houses.

O ver time, Callahan started to trust Jimmy enough to let him drive the company truck, after Jimmy got his California driver's license. Jimmy, with Callahan riding shotgun, would make deliveries and pick up supplies. Once they even dropped off film stock at the Keystone Studios where Mack Sennett made his comedies with Charlie Chaplin, W. C. Fields, and the Keystone Kops. Jimmy couldn't believe such a place where they made movies of people hitting each other, falling out of buildings, and throwing pies. It was controlled mayhem and everyone seemed to have a good time; if hearing Sennett yelling a lot and foaming at the mouth was considered a good time. When some actors cursed with the most God awful words on purpose with a straight face when saying their lines, it brought a smile to Jimmy's face. He realized, "Who would know unless you could read lips?"

Jimmy was feeling good about his life until that fateful day when he decided to figure out what all the hoopla was about and watched *The Birth of a Nation*. Now, he was angry, upset and started to get ideas for a photoplay of his own, one in which he would portray Negroes as decent, hard working, and wanting a strong family, the latter being something he had yearned for himself.

Over the next few months, Jimmy started buying photographic equipment from Callahan, often discarded equipment that he would refurbish on his own time. His once roomy apartment was now crowded with cameras, tripods, and lights. There was hardly any room to walk around. This had a dampening effect on his love life. While he did not find it difficult to find young women to go out with him—to dinners and to movies—once they saw his overcrowded apartment, they became scarce. The last one even said laughingly, "What a mess. Where's your mother?" Having only met Jimmy, she could be forgiven for such an insensitive remark. He felt like picking up her purse and flinging it out into the hall but he simply handed it to her and showed her the door. She was confused about the evening being cut short and left angrily mumbling about men. Leaning with his back on the door with his eyes closed, Jimmy whispered, "Yes, where are you?"

At work, during his lunch break, Jimmy took his first working movie camera outside and shot some test footage of passing traffic and pedestrians. Some people naturally shied away from him, others ignored him while others still smiled and waved. One young man even walked on his hands for the camera and asked while he was upside down where and when he could see it. Callahan had shown Jimmy how to develop print film and movie stock so that he could do that for Callahan's customers. With Callahan's permission, Jimmy developed his first footage at work and couldn't wait to get home to watch it.

He remembered the sheer joy he experienced the first time he projected it on a sheet in his living room. It was just life on Sunset Boulevard, the passers-by, the few automobiles, horse and buggies, the electric streetcar on tracks down the center of the street, the guy walking on his hands. The first footage was crap, overexposed, jumpy but none of that mattered. Jimmy made his first flicker. Over the next few weeks, he honed his skills at the camera and with lighting. He also learned how to develop film properly, like making sure the chemical baths to develop, stop, and fix was as close to 68 degrees Fahrenheit as possible. One or two degrees off, he found out, and the resultant film did not come out well. Finally, he was producing footage he would be proud to show others.

With his creative juices stirring, he started writing down ideas for a story. He needed a Negro man and woman to play the two lead parts. Fortunately, his new friend, George Baker, knew of a couple.

Jimmy had met George a few months before when George had a camera repaired at the shop. Near quitting time, George came by to pick it up. He walked up to a counter and handed a clerk a work order slip, and said, "I was told my camera would be fixed by now."

Not many Negroes came into the shop but the clerk saw that George was impeccably dressed. George, tall, of stocky build, was a traveling salesman. His outgoing personality and his penchant for three-piece suits would win over customers, black or white.

The clerk looked at the work order, and said, "Yes, sir." He checked various shelves and did not see it. "I'm sure it's here. Let me check in the back."

George nodded and bided his time by looking at stereoscopic slides in a viewer on display. George especially liked the views of the Yosemite Valley. He considered buying a viewer at some point, or even visiting the Valley.

The clerk walked into the repair shop, held up the work order, and shouted, "Camera for George Baker."

Jimmy was finishing polishing George's camera and looked up. "Right here."

The clerk hastily grabbed the camera from Jimmy. Jimmy protested, "Wait, don't you want to hear—"

The clerk was the one who brought in Jimmy that first day and had never warmed up to Jimmy. He turned his back, and said rudely, "The customer's waiting," and disappeared back into the store. Jimmy didn't care, shrugged, and started cleaning up his work area. Oops. There was George's lens cap sitting on his work bench. Jimmy picked it up and ran into the store.

Jimmy looked around, "George Baker?" No answer.

The rude clerk indicated the street. "He just left. Why?"

Holding up the cap, Jimmy said, "He forgot his lens cap."

The clerk pointed out the door, "Stocky nig— uh, gentleman in a three piece suit."

Jimmy ran out and looked around. He saw a man of the clerk's description and yelled, "George Baker!?"

George was just getting into his brand new car, a 1915 Lambert touring car, Model 48-C, convertible, top down. He looked up and said, "Yes."

"You forgot this." Jimmy held up his lens cap.

George looked at his camera and said, "Sure enough. Thank you."

Jimmy ran over and handed the cap to him and apologized.

George took the cap and snapped it over the lens. He said, "No harm done."

Jimmy took the time to admire the car. "This is one fine machine you have here."

"Thank you," George said as he amazed Jimmy by starting the car from the driver's seat with a newly patented electric starter. But he still had to coax it. "Come on, baby, come on, come on." It finally turned over but the idle was rough. "I just got this thing and damn if you don't need to handle it with kid gloves. Looks like I'll have to take it back to the garage again."

"Hold on for a minute, George," said Jimmy who ran back into the store. He returned with a screwdriver.

Jimmy requested, "Open the hood, please." George looked at him with skepticism. Jimmy explained, "Before I started working here, I worked in a car garage."

George got out and opened the hood. Jimmy got under the hood and made an adjustment to the carburetor with his screwdriver. The rough idle smoothed out.

George was appreciative. "Well, thank you, uh…"

"Jimmy, Jimmy Johnson."

After that, for helping George maintain his car, George let Jimmy drive the car when he was out of town which was often.

Once, after returning from a trip out of state, George came by Jimmy's apartment to retrieve his car. It was the first time that he had been there. He saw all the movie equipment crowded into the room. George said, "I love what you've done to the place. Are you in the wholesale business?"

Jimmy chuckled, "Yeah, I know it's a bit messy in here. I am looking for a bigger space. I'm going to make a moving picture."

George whistled in amazement. "Really?"

Jimmy asked, "You got a minute?"

"Yeah."

"Good." Jimmy moved a stack of books off the sofa to create a bare spot for George to sit. Jimmy then showed him the best of his Sunset Boulevard footage. George was impressed.

George asked, "Is that what you want to do—shoot street scenes of Hollywood?"

"No, I have a story in mind but I need a couple of actors, a man and woman, in their twenties or thirties who can work for cheap, like for nothing now, money later."

"Tall order but I think maybe Blake and Rose."

"Who?"

"Blake and Rose Thomas. Two part time community theater actors. Customers of mine. I could run it by them."

Excited, Jimmy jumped up, "That would be great!"

"I can't make any promises," George said as he got up to leave.

"Of course not."

George then put out his hand, and asked, "My car key?"

"Right." Jimmy fished the key out of his pocket and handed it to George.

Within a week, Jimmy found his new studio space in the Edendale District near Echo Park, not far from the Mack Sennett Studios. He saw a "For Rent" sign once while making deliveries for Sunset Camera.

It was a high ceiling artist's studio with large skylights, perfect for his moving picture work. A kitchen area in one corner, a wood stove in the opposite corner; the rest was open space except for a bathroom with a toilet and a tub in the back. He envisioned a small workshop on one wall, his bed on another. It was dusty with some leftover furniture. It even had an old upright piano with some missing keys that the owner of the building offered to remove. Jimmy asked to keep it.

Jimmy had learned to play the piano during down times on stage with his father and brother. Sometimes a kindly house piano player would consent to teach Jimmy a song or two. After a while, Jimmy became pretty good at tickling the ivories.

After moving into his new space, and making the place presentable, Jimmy invited Blake and Rose to share his vision of the moving picture he was making. Blake was tall, bearded, in his thirties, while Rose was a slender, pretty woman in her twenties. Although they didn't like not to get paid up front, being community theater performers, they were used to that. Jimmy promised money afterwards if his little picture made money. And the thought that they could be in a flicker brought them promise for more work and fame in the future. Jimmy photographed some test movie footage of them. When they saw it, they signed a simple contract and got started the following week.

During the spring and summer of 1916, Jimmy was well on his way to finishing his first short moving picture.

CHAPTER 10

ILLNESS AND DEATH

The morning after Reed kicked Jimmy out, Russell woke up with a hard knocking on his bedroom door. Reed opened the door sharply—he was already dressed—and said, "Get a move on, Russell, we got a train to catch."

What? Blearily, Russell searched his memory. Don't they have a show that night there in Chicago? He looked at Jimmy's unmade bed and felt a knot in the pit in his stomach. He thought, "What's Pop doing now?"

Rushing to catch the train, Russell asked his father, "What's going on?"

"We gotta make a new act. We'll do that in Detroit."

In Detroit, on the rehearsal stage, Reed was showing Russell how the new routine would be. It was a routine that he and Edgar developed. He didn't think Edgar would notice or care; hell, he didn't even know if Edgar was still alive. Russell had a hard time focusing. Reed knew why. He stopped and sat

Russell down on one of the bent wood caned chairs left on the stage. He crouched down and looked Russell in the eye.

"Russell, you've got to pay attention, son, if we are to make this work. Look, I admit, I may have been a bit harsh on Jimmy that night, but him quittin'—that came out of the blue. Did you know he wanted to leave?"

Russell looked at his dad, shook his head, and said, "No," although in hindsight he surely saw the signs.

"Well, you should be happy for Jimmy, shouldn't you? He wanted to leave the act, and he did."

Russell couldn't deny that simple truth, no matter how wrenching the parting. He took a deep breath, smiled, and said, "Okay, Pop. What do you got?"

Reed slapped Russell on the knee, and said, "Attaboy."

They worked hard that morning and afternoon to perfect their new act. That night, they previewed it to thunderous applause. As 'Perry and Johnson and Their Feets of Magic' so many years before, 'Johnson and Son' was a hit.

For seven more years, Reed and Russell traveled the Circuit. While Russell often thought of his brother and where he might be, the pain of that night in Chicago faded. Russell grew closer and closer to his dad.

Once, back in Chicago, in February of 1916, Reed fell ill to the flu. Reed was never sick but this time he was hit hard. For a week, Russell tended to Reed's every need, broth and crackers for food, cold compresses to abate the fever, trudging in a snowy blizzard to the local druggist for Bayer aspirin. Nothing seemed to help. Reed had always dreaded doctors and dentists, enduring toothaches until he had to have the tooth pulled. Despite all of Russell's efforts, Reed got weaker and weaker. Now he was coughing up blood. Russell had never seen his dad this way. Knowing that Reed was in no condition to argue, Russell bundled him up, and they took a taxicab to the hospital. They had never taken a cab before.

The emergency room was packed with coughing, feverish patients. Russell thought that if he didn't catch something himself, it would be a miracle. After a long wait with Reed coughing more and more, Russell's patience ran out and he started yelling at the admitting clerk for a doctor. An orderly had to subdue Russell but a doctor soon appeared. Taking Reed's temperature and listening to his lungs, the doctor immediately admitted Reed. Russell stayed the whole time in the hospital by his father's bed. With proper medication and attention, Reed finally started to improve. As soon as Reed could walk, he wanted out of the hospital. Russell had to use most of their savings to pay the bill.

When they first arrived in Chicago to start their engagement, before Reed got sick, theater manager Howard Bixby gave Reed a telegram from Sam, his brother out in California. Sam wanted them to come out there to headline shows in his new theater. Since they had never been to the West Coast before, he was sure that 'Johnson and Son' would be a hit. He would pay them extra. Russell was excited by the prospect but was disappointed when Reed wired Sam, "Thanks but no thanks." He told Russell that he wanted to stay with what was tried and true. Reed said, "After all, if it ain't broke, why fix it?" Russell was disappointed. He wanted to see what California was all about.

After a few more days to let Reed fully recover from his illness, they returned to the theater and found Howard in his office.

Howard was happy to see them and said, "Hey, Reed, we missed you around here."

"Been sick as hell. Almost bought the farm." Reed slaps Russell on the back. "Russell here saved me—he had to take me to the hospital. I hate hospitals and it cost us a bundle. But we're as good as new and rarin' to go. You got extra shows we can do?"

"Glad to have you back—oh, oops, I almost forgot." The manager opened a desk drawer and took out a telegram which he handed to Reed. "This came for you."

"What? From Sam again? I thought I told him..." Reed's voice trailed as he read the telegram, then, softly, "Oh, Jesus."

Concerned, Russell said, "Pop, what's the matter?"

Reed shoved the telegram to Russell, and said, "It's from your grandmother."

Russell read out loud, "Your father very ill. Stop. Come home immediately. Stop—"

Reed asked Howard, "When did you get this?"

Howard replied, "About a week ago."

"Dammit! Come on, Russell." He looked at the manager and said, "Howard, we got to go."

"Understand. Let me pay what I owe you." Howard reached into a cash box from a safe and gave Reed his pay. He and Reed shook hands. Howard said, "Good luck."

"Thanks." With that, he and Russell rushed back to their hotel, packed, and left on the next train for Memphis.

That trip took three more days with delays for snow. When they arrived, it was too late. Reed and Russell arrived in time for the funeral. Damn! The flu that gripped Reed took his father. Lethe cried when Reed and Russell burst through the door to the funeral home brushing snow off their overcoats. Reed hugged his mother for a long time.

Reed had always been stoic, hard as nails, but when he saw his father's peaceful face in the open casket, he cried as he had never cried before. Russell, tears streaming down his face, had never seen his father in so much emotional pain. He held his father by his shoulders. Reed was heaving with grief and repeatedly walked to the casket and back to the chairs.

After the service, at their house, many relatives, friends, and barber shop customers came to pay their respects. Reed thanked each one.

Reed and Russell stayed around for a few days more to help Lethe cope with their loss. Fortunately, Aunt Harriet, a sister of Lethe's, had offered to move in with her. One afternoon, Reed went into their back yard. Even winter barren and with a light blanket of snow, Reed could see that the yard was wildly overgrown and had been unkempt for years. He could hardly recognize it as the site of his and Miriam's wedding. That brought back memories of that terrible night when Miriam disgraced the family and he had to take the boys away. He got angry again. Damn her! Damn her! At least, he thought, there was a measure of relief that Jimmy wasn't around anymore to torment him about what happened that night. Russell was too young to remember and he never brought it up. That was all right by Reed.

Lethe asked Reed a question that he struggled with for a long time after. After the reception with most visitors gone and some helping to clean up, Lethe was sitting in her rocking chair in the parlor with Reed and Russell on the sofa. She stopped rocking and leaned forward. She had to ask, "Reed, will I see Jimmy?"

Reed knew this subject would come up eventually and dreaded it. He said, "I don't know. In Chicago a while back, Jimmy decided not to be a hoofer anymore. He wanted out of the act. He left and... and we don't know where he is."

She leaned back in her rocker and said calmly, "You don't know where he is." Lethe let this settle in, and then surmised, "Let me guess. You didn't give him your blessing."

Lethe saw Russell silently shaking his head, "no." Reed avoided her gaze, feeling like the little boy from his childhood who got caught with his hand in the cookie jar. Looking down on the carpet, he focused on the pattern, and said, "Not exactly..."

"You mean you got mad as hell," she said as she glared at him.

Reed nodded. Lethe continued rocking back and forth a bit before leaning forward once again and took Reed's hand. She said, "Reed, isn't what Jimmy did to you the same thing you did to your father and me when you took off with Edgar Perry?"

That hit Reed like a ton of bricks. He never looked at it that way.

She continued, "We had our doubts. We didn't want you to go. But we knew that it was something you had to do. So, we gave you our blessing. It was like when your father and I decided to leave the Johnson plantation and come to Memphis. Son, each person has to find their own way."

Tears started to well up in Reed's eyes. Had he been too harsh? Had he been too selfish, only thinking of himself? That night, Reed had fits with bad dreams swirling in his head. He woke up thinking that he had to make it up to his oldest.

Lethe wanted to sell James' closed-up barber shop since it was obvious that Reed would not or could not take it over. She sent her son and grandson to clean it up for prospective buyers. Armed with brooms, feather dusters, buckets and mops, they opened up the musky shop. It was all there as Reed had remembered, the two barber chairs, bottles of shampoo and bars of shaving soap lining a shelf, old newspapers still stacked in the waiting area. It even had a poster of a vaudeville bill showing 'Johnson and Son' headlining.

Reed rubbed a finger on the leather top of a barber chair and picked up a layer of dust. It brought back memories of when he was a boy and his father tried to teach him the ways of the shop. Lots of customers, lots of camaraderie and laughter.

It was so alive. Now, nothing. Even the pendulum clock on the wall had stopped. Reed checked his father's pocket watch, reset the clock time, and pushed the pendulum. Tick, tock, tick, tock as he and Russell dusted, swept, washed, and tossed out two barrels of debris.

In a few days, they had sold the shop. It gave Lethe some money to live on. Reed promised to send as much money as he could afford. When Reed saw the new owner of the barber shop take down his father's sign and replace it with his own, Reed felt bad that he couldn't have done what his father wanted him to do—to keep the shop in the family.

After two weeks in Memphis, Reed and Russell had to get back to work. They needed money, not only for themselves but now for Lethe. In his old bedroom in his parent's house that he shared with Russell, Reed came across the telegram from Sam that offered to headline them in California at a bigger than normal salary. In addition, on the Circuit, while they were good, he felt they had gotten stale. Perhaps on the West Coast they could rejuvenate. So, it surprised the hell out of Russell when Reed announced that they would take Sam up and try California.

Reed telegraphed Sam and asked if his offer was still good.

He got his answer the next day: "More than ever!" Reed and Russell started packing. Russell was ecstatic, like a kid again.

The next morning, they kissed Lethe good-bye and boarded the Union Pacific. They traveled through Texas, New Mexico, Arizona, and finally, into California. On this long train ride with time to think, Reed had come to rationalize that he had made the right decision about Jimmy. Jimmy wanted to leave, and he left. Jimmy broke up a terrific act. Sure, he and Russell were good but the three of them were dynamite. It would be hard to forgive Jimmy for that.

A smiling Sam met them at the train station. It was like old times again. Thus, in the spring of 1916, Reed and Russell found themselves headlining at the Roxie Theater in Los Angeles, not far from either Jimmy or Miriam.

CHAPTER 11

PHOTOPLAYS

Hollywood, California (1916). Jimmy was setting up the next shot in his studio with Blake and Rose in costume. A bright and sunny day, the skylights provided all the light that he needed.

Standing at the front door of Jimmy's studio, to the left was his workbench for his tools and paints. A storage area held some movie props. In the far left corner there was an ice box and kitchen area with a gas stove. A round table with three mismatched chairs completed his "dining room." On the back wall, next to the sink was his pantry. To the right of it were his wardrobe and a twin size bed. A makeshift bookshelf held his books. A back door leading to an unkempt yard was blocked with more movie props, not only for security but because he needed the space. In the corner was his restroom and bathtub. Along the right wall, under the large array of skylights Blake and Rose stood anxiously waiting in the living room set consisting of a small sofa, a coffee table, a chair, and a floor lamp.

A large canvas wall hanging of draped windows and potted plants behind them completed the illusion. A movie camera in the middle of the room pointed toward his actors. In the near corner on the right there was a wood stove and a small wood pile for heating the building. With a long pole with a hook, he could open the skylights on hot summer days. Next to the front door were the old upright piano and a white sheet on the wall for his movie screen. A movie projector in the middle of the room pointed to the sheet.

Jimmy got behind his movie camera and looked through the lens. He wore pants with suspenders and his tweed driver cap turned backwards. He drew a chalk line from the back wall on the hardwood floor on the left side of the set back to the left side of the camera. He checked the view through the camera again and drew another line from the back wall on the floor on the right side of the set back to the right side of the camera. Pointing to the two lines making a cone, he said to his actors, "Be sure to stay inside those lines or you'll be out of camera range."

Blake and Rose looked on the floor and impatiently got into their positions. Blake said, "Okay, we get it, Jimmy. Let's get it going."

Jimmy asked, "You know the scene?"

"Yes!" they both exclaimed. Jimmy looked through the lens and started cranking the camera handle. "Go."

"You come in at 2 in the morning," Blake exclaimed. "What am I to think!?"

Rose got into his face. "Ha! What about you? You get to stay out all night!!"

"That's different, woman."

"Different?"

All through this byplay, Jimmy gave direction and encouragement. "Good. Excellent. Into his face more, Rose."

Suddenly, they heard a snap and one corner of the background canvas fell, revealing the unpainted wall behind. Jimmy and his actors looked at the blank wall. Jimmy stopped cranking the camera. "Dammit!" he barked.

Rose smothered a chuckle while Blake just shook his head. Jimmy was not amused.

"Come on, Jimmy," Blake said, "I'll get the ladder."

Across town, Griffith was preparing to film on his newly constructed Babylonian set. On the back wall, two dozen extras, all men, were perched over 100 feet in the air. A flock of seagulls flew past them at eye level. The extras were dressed in Babylonian costumes, and most wore false beards. Incongruously, one of the extras was smoking a cigar.

Erich von Stroheim, the future director and actor, famous as the butler, Max, in Billy Wilder's *Sunset Boulevard*, was one of Griffith's young assistants. He was similarly dressed in a Babylonian costume. In his trademark Teutonic accent, he shouted out, "All right, gentlemen. We are about to begin—" He saw the stogie, and demanded, "Hey, you! Get rid of that cigar!"

The extra remarked, "What for? The Old Man can't see it—" He pointed to the front of the set. "Shit, he's so far away, we could be jacking off back here and he wouldn't know it." He indicated so as the others laughed.

von Stroheim, not laughing, started toward the defiant extra with a stern face.

"All right!" The extra relented and tossed the cigar over the wall to the street below.

von Stroheim spoke and the extras obeyed without question. "Positions, everyone! Wait for the signal."

Outside the set, Edgar Perry, now in tattered clothes, unshaven, dejected, happened by when the tossed cigar plopped down near him. He looked up and saw the skeletal scaffolding work that supported the wall. Smiling, he picked up the cigar, flicked off some dirt, and took a long draw, savoring the taste. He was just fired from being an extra on the set. He had worked a couple of days and made a few dollars but missed two days due to drinking and sleeping it off. Griffith's people had no time for such shenanigans and said they didn't need him anymore. Had he worked there longer, he and Miriam might have recognized each other. Or not, as it had been over twenty years since their last encounter and she went by "Helen," not "Miriam."

He tried his luck at other studios in Hollywood hawking himself as a song and dance man but got no offers. He suspected his appearance did not help. He tried to look presentable but who could afford clean clothes? Ah, who needed them, anyway? He decided to go back to his digs on South Central Avenue where he could dance in bars for tips.

After being thrown out at Reed and Miriam's wedding, Edgar wandered the streets of Memphis drinking and feeling sorry for himself. He would steal glimpses of the act Reed and Miriam were putting together. He got more and more angry, and thought it best to leave town before something ugly happened.

He tried to resurrect his solo act but found that he had relied on Reed to provide the spark to keep going. Besides, wasn't it easier to drink the day away than to work?

Edgar lived a meager existence, getting work when he could. With little or no money, Edgar traveled by hopping on freight trains. Always a dicey proposition because you don't know who else you would meet up, mean folks on both sides of the law. Until 1915, he was lucky with having mild confrontations on only a few occasions but this time, his luck ran out. With only a few dollars left in his pocket, Edgar ran after an accelerating train. He reached for the open doorway of the freight car. A hand reached out and offered to pull him on board. Wary, he made a quick decision to grab the hand. He was grateful to get inside until he saw four rough looking fellow passengers. He saw they were trouble but before he could jump off, they jumped him and gave him a severe beating and he passed out.

When he finally woke up, he felt bruises but no cuts or broken bones. He ran his tongue over his teeth. Damn! He lost a front tooth. Who were those bastards? Suddenly, he thought they could still be in the car. He jumped up and backed into a corner, looking about the car. He was relieved to find he was alone. He looked out at the passing scenery—sand and cacti with jagged mountains in the distance. Where was he and how long had he been out? He checked his pockets and found what little money he had was gone. After another day and night, the train slowed down and stopped in a large train yard. What city was this? He heard railroad officers—bulls—hitting the cars with baseball bats trying to roust illegal riders.

He didn't need any more beatings and slipped out before they reached his car. One bull chased him but he managed to jump over a fence and run across a road. He made it downtown and found he was in California, in Los Angeles. He had never been in the state before.

For the first few days, he scrounged garbage cans for food, and found a cardboard box and old newspapers for bedding. He wasn't welcome in most parts of town but found it more hospitable on South Central Avenue. He found one tavern, the Nite Owl, which gave him lunch for entertaining the customers. This he could do. He soon became aware of the Roxie Theater in the neighborhood, and went to see if he could resurrect his act. This was a few months before Reed and Russell would arrive.

He cleaned up best as he could, washed his clothes in the Los Angeles River, and borrowed a razor from the owner of the Nite Owl. He really needed this job.

He found Sam Bixby, now sporting a moustache, in his office. Sam looked up from his paperwork.

Edgar asked, "You the manager?"

Sam leaned back in his chair, and said, "Manager and owner."

Edgar said, "I'm a hoofer from way back and I would like a chance to perform again on stage."

"Looks like you've hit on hard times."

He looked at himself and cringed, thinking, "Damn. And I thought I cleaned up myself pretty good." He said to Sam, "That I have. But I still have the moves."

Edgar demonstrated some dance steps. Sam was impressed and was leaning to give him a shot. He picked up a pencil and asked, "What's your name?"

"Perry. Edgar Perry."

Sam tapped the pencil a few times on the paper. He knew who he was from the stories Reed told him. Reed never revealed what happened with Miriam but he never had a kind word for his old dance partner. Sam said, "Sorry, Mr. Perry. I just don't have anything open right now."

There was fire in Edgar's eyes when he said, "Why the hell why not? Winter's coming on and I need the work. I can do this."

Sam stood up, and said, "Hey, I hear a hundred sob stories every day. I don't have to explain anything to you. Get out!"

Edgar did, slamming Sam's office door behind him. Sam hadn't thought about Reed for a while but according to his brother back in Chicago, 'Johnson and Son' was very popular. He wondered if he could lure Reed out to the West Coast. He would be a genuine headliner, a guaranteed moneymaker. He went right away to the telegraph office and wired a message for Reed through his brother.

After being rejected by Sam, Edgar cursed that he went to so much trouble to wash his suit and to shave. Sure, there were other theaters he could try but what was the use? How many times did he need to be kicked in the teeth? That evening, he went back to the Nite Owl, got a few tips from dancing, and bought a bottle of whiskey. He went to his alley and proceeded to lie down on his makeshift bed and drink the whole bottle. Even if his outsides were cold, his insides were warm.

CHAPTER 12

A GYPSY PRESENCE

Back at the Babylonian set, if someone walked the half-mile length from the back wall where von Stroheim and his extras stood to the front, they would pass under set pieces of propped up plastered walls every three or four hundred feet. Along the journey, they would pass through the hundreds of Babylonian dressed extras, men and women.

They would then pass under the central arch, past the great plaster elephants sitting on pedestals that Griffith had approved earlier in the carpenter shop, the great open court, down the long, wide stairway to the front of the set to where Griffith stood. When they turned around, they would stand in awe of the grandeur of Griffith's giant diorama—the Feast of Belshazzar. And true enough, they would barely discern von Stroheim and his extras.

On a platform facing the set, D. W. Griffith, in a suit and tie, wearing a wide-brimmed hat, held a large megaphone. At 41, he was at the height of his filmmaking abilities. Next to him were his assistants: his long-time cameraman, Billy Bitzer, Mr. Slocum, a heavy set man in his thirties holding a pistol at his side, and young Karl, taking notes on a clipboard.

Behind them floated a large helium-filled publicity balloon with a woven basket hanging below tethered to about fifty feet of rope. On the face of the balloon was a huge banner which stated, *Mother and the Law*, the original title for his photoplay. Griffith started to make *Mother and the Law*, a then modern day story about injustice, shortly after finishing *The Birth of a Nation*. When the furor over the racist aspects of *Birth* surprised and overwhelmed Griffith, he decided to answer his critics by adding three more stories of injustice to his picture.

Griffith, anxious to get the day's shooting started, asked his cameraman, "Billy, are you ready?"

"Whenever you are, Mr. Griffith."

Griffith nodded to his other assistant, "Mr. Slocum..."

Slocum raised the pistol in the air to fire a shot to signal all the extras and assistants to start the action. Bitzer started hand cranking his camera.

Suddenly, Griffith realized, "Wait! Where are the girls on the stairs?" All looked to see the empty staircase. "Karl, get to the barn and find out what's keeping them, please."

"Yes, sir." Karl set his clipboard down, and then took off running. Billy stopped cranking. Slocum lowered his gun. Griffith fell back into a chair, frustrated.

At his studio, Jimmy was up on a ladder that Blake held. He had nailed up the fallen corner of the canvas with conviction.

"There. That should do it," Jimmy said.

He heard another snap and the other corner of the canvas fell down. "Dammit!" Jimmy wanted to smash the hammer into the wall but caught himself.

Karl ran across the street from the set to the studio lot where he entered the costume barn. A dozen dressers were fitting dozens of girls, all in their early twenties, into their Babylonian costumes.

Karl ran in, out of breath. "Mr. Griffith needs the girls—NOW!"

Sophie finished working on her girl and said, "Okay, Karl, don't get your knickers into a twist." She looked up at the other dressers. "How are we doing?"

The other dressers answered,

"Done."

"Got it, Sophie."

"Finished."

Sophie said, "You got 'em, Karl."

Karl, never one to displease Griffith, waved his arms wildly in a circular motion as a windmill in a thunderstorm. "Come on, girls, hurry! Hurry!"

The costumed girls ran out with him. The dressers finally had a chance to relax. One, Doris, a younger girl, plopped down on a chair exhausted, waving a prop fan over her face, relieved the chaos was over for now.

Away from the hustle and bustle in the main room, in a dressing room, Helen helped Lillian Gish out of her costume. *Intolerance* consisted of four intertwining stories from different periods of history. Gish, one of the stars in *The Birth of a Nation*, played a relatively minor role in this film, that of a mother rocking a cradle in a scene which signaled a transition from one story to the next. Griffith had filmed her part earlier that morning.

Helen helped Gish into her street clothes. Gish then sat down at a mirror and started powdering her face. She said, "Unless Mr. Griffith needs me for another part, I think I'm through for this picture."

Helen looked disappointed. Gish said, "Oh, don't worry, there will be plenty of work here for you." Helen knew that but wanted to work with Gish more.

Gish asked, "What brought you to California, Helen? Your boys?"

In the mirror's reflection, Gish saw Helen grasp her locket and take a deep breath. She stopped powdering, turned to Helen, and said, "Oh, I'm sorry. I just thought by now..."

Helen replied, "No, that's okay. No... no news, I'm afraid. I'll be all right."

Gish took Helen by the hand and said, "In any case, we're glad you're here."

In the main room, a flamboyantly dressed and scarfed Negro woman, Madame Sul-te-Wan, in her early forties looking more gypsy than not, marched in with authority. Charismatic and assured, though not with much formal schooling, she could quickly read people and situations and often put others on the defense.

Loudly, she said, "You ladies ready for the next costume change?" She clapped her hands repeatedly, and laughed. "Let's go, let's go!"

Having worked with Griffith for two years, Madame knew most of the dressers well. In good nature, they yelped and booed, then went about their business.

Madame spotted Sophie and said, "Miss Sophie, I'm ready for my fitting."

"Oh, I gave that to Helen, the new girl. Check with her." Sophie looked about the room and pointed, "I think she's helping Miss Gish in number 5."

In the dressing room, Gish and Helen heard a knock on the door. Gish turned toward it, and said, "Yes?"

Madame opened the door and said, "Good afternoon, Miss Gish." She now saw Helen and said, "Oh, you must be Miss Helen?"

"Yes, and please, you can just call me Helen."

Gish introduced, "Helen, this is Madame Sul-te-wan, an actress here."

Helen looked impressed. Madame took a deep bow. Gish said, "What is it, Madame?"

"Miss Sophie says that Helen here supposed to fit my costume for my big scene next week."

Gish turned back toward the mirror and continued to powder her face. Looking in the mirror at Madame, Gish said, "She's quite busy right now. It will have to wait."

Despite Madame being nearly twice the age of Gish, Madame understood her place, and said without rancor, "Of course, it can." She now looked at Helen, "Are you busy... Friday?"

Helen said, "Check with Sophie but I think I can help you then."

Madame said, "Very wonderful. Ladies." Madame smiled broadly, and left, backing away and closing the door. Out in the main room, Helen and Gish heard Madame say, "You all don't work so hard, hear?" She could be heard laughing heartily as the dressers laughed with her.

Helen asked, "Is 'Madame' her real name?"

Gish said, "Mr. Griffith calls her 'Nellie' but how she got the name, 'Madame,' no one here is bold enough to ask." They both giggled.

CHAPTER 13

WEST COAST PREMIERE

At his workbench of tools, cans of paints, and brushes, Jimmy was hand lettering title cards, white paint on black paper. Title cards in a silent movie displayed unheard dialogue or plot explanations. Though talented in many other ways, Jimmy was not very good at lettering or judging how to space the words. He was sloppy with letters often crammed at the end of the paper. He had to toss more cards on the floor than he kept, cursing each time.

Interrupted by a knock on his front door, Jimmy got up and answered. A telegraph boy handed Jimmy a telegram. Jimmy gave the boy a penny tip, closed the door, and opened the message.

It was from George who sent it from Seattle, Washington. It read,

GOOD NEWS STOP FOUND MIRIAM JOHNSON HERE WHO MOVED TO CALIFORNIA STOP WILL

CHECK BAY AREA STOP BACK HOME IN THREE
DAYS

Jimmy smiled but didn't allow himself to get overexcited.
He had gone through too many disappointments before. He
looked up on the wall above his workspace at the tintype photograph that he'd looked at a thousand times before—that of
his mother, smiling, happy at Coney Island. He sighed and
went back to work.

When Jimmy moved into his new studio space, George
used his car to help him transport his things. Jimmy also
borrowed the truck from Sunset Camera for some of the larger
pieces of movie equipment and furniture. After Jimmy settled
in, George came by and saw the photo of Jimmy's mother on
the wall. He pointed to it, "Who's she? Your girlfriend?"

Jimmy had to smile, and said, "No, my mother, taken
twenty years ago."

George smirked and said, "Oops, don't I feel foolish?"

Jimmy said, "I'm looking for her. I haven't seen her since
I was five."

George sat down, and asked, "What the hell happened?"

Jimmy shook his head and said, "I wish I knew." He
then went on to tell George what he knew of the night she
left. He told of him tracking her to his grandparent's house

in Baltimore. Even with the new owner's belongings in the house, he felt her presence. He was sure she was still out there, somewhere, and he needed to find her to find out what really happened that night.

George took out a small notebook, and asked her name. He wrote down "Miriam Johnson." George said, "In my job I travel a lot. I can make inquiries."

Jimmy's face brightened as he shook George's hand, and said, "That would be swell."

As evening descended, street lights and headlights illuminated the one-mile commercial district known as the South Central Corridor. People of color were going in and out of diners, taverns, and the Roxie Theater. The marquee heralded the first West Coast appearance of 'Johnson and Son.'

Inside, on stage, a poster on an easel announced 'Johnson and Son.' Sam Bixby, peeking from offstage, saw that the house was packed. He smiled and metaphorically patted himself on the back for his instincts about headlining his old friends. Reed and Russell were dressed alike, tap dancing in their trademarked suits, derbies, and canes. A piano player played the accompanying music.

Although Russell was young and energetic, he had a hard time keeping up with his fifty-year-old father. At one point, they both threw their canes in the air. Reed, seemingly without looking, caught his cane on its way down. And though Russell had done this hundreds of times before, he dropped his. This elicited a gasp from the crowd as Russell picked up his cane and continued, not wanting to interrupt the routine. However, Reed glared at his son for the error. Russell shrugged an apology. With their show over, they bowed to raucous applause, the audience having forgotten about the dropped cane. Reed did not.

As they left the stage, Russell said, "Sorry, Pop."

Reed only replied, "We'll work on it." Reed looked up and saw two square holes, one larger than the other, cut out in the back wall above the audience's heads. Painters were busy painting the room behind. He pointed it out to Russell, and said, "What the—"

Backstage, Reed ran into Sam. Sam shook Reed's hand and said, "Wonderful, boys, just wonderful."

Reed said, "Hey, Sam, I'd say you got some mighty big rats here."

"Huh? Where?" Sam looked around on the floor.

Reed gave Sam a gentle tap on a shoulder. He said, pointing, "No, up there, those two holes in the back wall..."

Relieved, Sam replied, "Oh, that. Just tryin' to survive. I'm adding moving pictures to the repertoire."

Reed slapped his forehead and said in disbelief, "Moving pictures? Not you too? Don't you theater owners understand that people want to see real people on stage, not "moving pictures?" I've been in this business for over thirty years—believe me, vaudeville is the ticket—it will be here forever. Am I right, Russell?"

Sam shrugged, not so sure. Neither was Russell as he said, "Sure, Pop." He and Reed left as the next act got started. Sam took this opportunity between acts to walk up the aisle to check out the progress of his new projection booth.

NOT FORGIVEN

A t Sunset Camera, Jimmy was intently repairing a torn-apart camera on his workbench when Callahan stepped out of his glass-encased office. He peered among his half-dozen craftsmen, and yelled, "Ferguson!"

A fellow worker replied, "Not here, Boss—throwing up. Can't lay off the booze."

"Dammit! He keeps that shit up, he's going to get his ass fired." Callahan looked around the room. "Jimmy!"

Jimmy looked up. "Sir!"

"You drive. Help me with the Prestwich." Callahan stood next to a large 35 mm projector for commercial use. He, Jimmy, and another employee loaded the heavy and bulky machine into the back of the camera shop truck. With ropes, they tied it securely to the truck bed. Callahan tossed Jimmy the keys.

Jimmy smiled as he got in behind the wheel while Callahan hand cranked the truck engine. When the engine turned over,

Jimmy pressed on the gas pedal to keep it going. Callahan opened the passenger side door and got in.

Jimmy asked, "Where to, Boss?"

Callahan wiped his hands clean on a red rag and said, "The Roxie Theater, on South Central." He tossed the rag onto the floor. "Get out on Sunset, and turn right."

After a twenty minute drive, Jimmy found himself lumbering down the avenue towards the theater. Callahan pointed, "There it is."

Jimmy looked up. He could not help but see the marquee proclaiming, "Johnson and Son. First West Coast Appearance! Limited Engagement."

"Watch it!" Callahan yelled.

Jimmy was so intent on the marquee that he almost smashed into the car stopped in front of him. He slammed on the brakes.

"What's the matter with you!?"

Before Jimmy could explain, Callahan pointed, "Quick, grab that spot right in front." Jimmy deftly maneuvered and pulled into the open space. He put the truck into neutral, yanked on the parking brake, and turned off the engine.

He and Callahan got out. Sam came out of the theater. Callahan went to him and shook his hand, "Morning." They went to look at the Prestwich. Sam gently stroked the projector, remarking, "It's a beauty."

"You got the best."

"I sure hope this works—it's costing me a bundle."

"You won't regret it. You got someone to help us?"

"Yeah, sure," Sam said as he turned to go inside to get some help.

Callahan looked around for his driver and found him looking at the list of acts on the posted playbill. Of course, he focused on 'Johnson and Son.' Jimmy muttered, "Could it be?" He then looked about the neighborhood and saw only people of color. He thought, "A good place to show my picture." He would ask the theater owner.

Callahan yelled out, "Hey, Jimmy! What the hell are you doing? Get over here."

"Right away, Boss." Jimmy ran over and started helping Callahan untie the projector.

Inside the theater, going up a flight of stairs, Callahan, Jimmy, and a theater janitor struggled to get the huge projector into the newly built projection booth.

The three men jockeyed the projector into place with the lens pointing toward the larger opening in the wall. Sam walked in to watch the progress.

Callahan wiped sweat off his brow. "Okay, Jimmy, now you can take five. Hey, Sam, good. Where's your electrical?"

Sam pointed, "Right there." Callahan started laying out cable lines.

At the sound of his voice, Jimmy spun around to face Sam. He asked, "Sam? Sam Bixby?" Sam looked different in his moustache.

It took Sam a moment to recognize Jimmy who had physically matured not just from the passage of time but from the struggles he had to endure for being on his own. Jimmy put out his hand and they shook.

Sam said, "Jimmy, Jimmy Johnson. Whew! It's been, what, seven years now, back in Chicago. Are you working for Callahan?"

Jimmy answered, "I am—fixing cameras. That's right. Your brother said you were opening a theater in California."

"He told me you got out of the business."

"I'm happier now. Listen, while I have you here, I myself am making a moving picture—"

This surprised Sam, "You? Really?"

Callahan looked over and shrugged like "Who knew?"

Jimmy continued, "Not long, a one-reeler."

Sam dug into his vest pocket for a business card. He handed it to Jimmy. "Bring it by when it's done. If I like it, I'll be happy to show it. We can talk business then."

Jimmy could hardly contain his excitement. "I know you're going to love it." He then said, "Sam. I saw 'Johnson and Son' headlining. That wouldn't be—"

"Your father and brother? It is."

Excited, Jimmy asked, "Do you know where I can find them?"

Sam looked out the smaller projector opening toward the stage. Jimmy now heard faint dance steps. Sam pointed. Jimmy looked through the opening in the wall and saw two familiar figures practicing. He almost jumped.

Breathing heavily, Jimmy said, "Boss, I'll be back in a minute." Callahan, intent on his electrical work, just mumbled in reply.

On stage, Reed and Russell, in more casual clothes, practiced the routine from the night before. They both threw their canes in the air and both caught them.

Reed said, "Once more—"

They stopped when they heard a lone clapping from the dimly lit empty theater.

Jimmy remarked, "You haven't lost the touch, I see."

Russell was jubilant, "Jimmy! Pop, it's Jimmy!" Reed surprised himself by not being overjoyed to see his first born. It only reminded him how hard he and Russell had to work without him. He was stoic as ever. Russell jumped down to the floor and hugged his brother.

Reed stepped down too. Jimmy gave him a hug that Reed did not return. Jimmy saw from his body language and facial expression that Reed still showed disdain for his son. Jimmy cautiously said, "Happy to see you, Pop."

Already knowing the answer, with a false smile, Reed said, "Have you finally come to your senses, boy, and come to re-join the act?"

Jimmy paused, then looked Reed straight in the eye and replied, "You know I can't."

Reed nodded, "Thought so."

Jimmy said exuberantly, "Pop, I'm making a moving picture. And... and... Sam here might show it." Jimmy's enthusiasm got Russell excited.

In reply, Reed angrily said, "That's just great. First you quit the act, and now you want to put us out of business with this newfangled moving picture crap!"

Jimmy tried to explain, "No, I don't want to put you out of business. You don't understand. I... I got a job just like I said I would. And I just want to show you what I'm doing—"

Reed said, "Got no time for no tomfoolery. Russell and I got real work to do." He turned around and went back up to the stage.

Jimmy's shoulders sagged as he looked at his brother, and sighed, "He still hates me, doesn't he?"

"He doesn't. He just doesn't understand you. Listen, I want to see your picture."

Jimmy brightened, "Yes, good. I'm on Alvarado at Beverly." Jimmy hesitated, knowing that what he had to say was not Russell's favorite topic. "Um, I may have a tip on Mom—"

True enough, Russell got sullen and said, "Do we have to do this again? When are you going to stop wasting your time? Accept the fact that she's gone. For all we know, she's dead and buried."

Jimmy continued, in a low voice, "Don't say that. I know what I saw at the train station. Pop hasn't told us the whole truth."

Russell looked back at Reed who was not paying attention, and said quietly but forcefully to Jimmy, "And like the fellow said, 'There's the rub.' We may never know the truth. Hell, I don't even remember our mother. I wouldn't know her if she were standing here right next to us!"

"I have her photograph—"

"That old thing? Taken twenty years ago. All I know is that she left us and never came back."

"Did she leave us or did we leave her?"

"That's bullshit."

"I know what I saw—"

Reed called from the stage, impatiently, "Russell! Get up here!"

From an opening in the projection booth, Callahan called out, "Jimmy! Ready to test this baby. Get the reel from the truck."

Jimmy and Russell parted. Russell then stopped, turned around toward his brother, and said, "Hey!" Jimmy turned. Russell, now more conciliatory, smiled, and said, "Take care."

Jimmy smiled back.

Reed shouted, "Russell!"

Now, Callahan, "Jimmy!"

Russell bolted for the stage while Jimmy ran back up the aisle. Russell and Reed restarted their routine. After a short time, the curtains opened behind them to reveal a giant motion picture screen rolling down. The stage lights went dimmer. Reed and Russell stopped. Reed glared at the booth, stomping off stage and cursing. Russell followed.

CHAPTER 15

MAKING NEW FRIENDS

A few days later, George walked up to Jimmy's studio. He saw his car parked in front. He gave it a once over and was pleased to see no damage. He gave it a friendly pat. He had returned from Seattle, having stopped in the Bay Area to find clues about Jimmy's mother. He wished he had good news.

Jimmy had just finished editing his picture when he heard George's knock on his door.

"George! Your timing's perfect. Come in." Jimmy said excitedly. "Have I got something to show you."

Jimmy darkened the room and threaded the film in the projector. Proudly, he said, "Be prepared to be amazed." He started hand cranking the projector. Between the flickering images of his actors, a number of Jimmy's sloppily hand-lettered title cards appeared. The last two proved especially hard to read:

- You come in at 2 in the morning. What am I to think!?

- Ha! What about you? You stay out all night!!

The last filmed scene ended abruptly, leaving a blinding white rectangle on the sheet screen. Jimmy turned off the projector and opened the shades.

"I have only two more scenes to finish. I even got a theater that might show it. What do you think, George?"

George tried to be diplomatic, "The picture's good, damned good. I like Blake and Rose. One thing, though..."

"Yes..."

"I have to tell you, the title cards are shit. I could barely read them."

"I... I did the best I could."

George reached into his coat inside pocket and took out his wallet. "I understand but if you want to sell this thing, get the cards done right." He handed Jimmy ten dollars. "Prospect Printing, on La Brea. Tell Henry I sent you. He'll give you a deal."

Jimmy pocketed the money, and said, "Hey, my first investor."

George smiled, and got up. Jimmy took the key to the Lambert from his pocket and gave it to George.

George asked, "How's it doing?"

"Purrin' like a kitten. I gave it an oil change and tuned it."

"Much obliged."

Almost afraid to ask, Jimmy inquired, "I'm guessing, up north, you didn't find my mother."

George shook his head, and said, "Not in 'Frisco or Oakland. But I know a guy here who works in the Hall of Records. He'll let me do some digging." Seeing how disappointed Jimmy was, George said, "Chin up. A landlord up there in Seattle said that the Miriam Johnson he rented to matched your mom's age and description. And she came from the East Coast. If she's in Los Angeles, we'll find her."

Outside, Jimmy smiled as he watched George drive off. He fed off of George's confidence and for the first time in a long time, he felt hope.

At Prospect Printing, one of a handful of successful Negro owned businesses in Hollywood, a woman in her early twenties, named Anita Pritchard, listened to a Dictaphone through headphones while nimbly typing on an Underwood. She sat in an outer office with a filing cabinet, a calendar, and a candlestick telephone on her desk. The overhead door bell jangled when Jimmy walked in, carrying a wrapped bundle.

Anita barely heard the bell, looked up, and saw Jimmy walking in. She turned off the Dictaphone, removed the

headphones, stood up, and walked towards him. He set his
bundle on the counter that separated them.

Anita said, "Hello. May I help you?"

"Yes, I'm to see... Henry."

"And you are?"

"Jimmy. Jimmy Johnson."

"Wait here, please."

Anita turned and walked through a door in the back. He
eyed her as she disappeared into the back room. Slim, attractive, he liked what he saw. Through the door left open,
Jimmy could see and hear the noisy printing presses in the
main work area.

Anita emerged with Henry, a Negro man in his forties,
short and stocky. He was wearing a black printer's apron and
wire-rimmed glasses. Anita sat back down to her typewriter
and re-read her work.

Seeing Jimmy, Henry inquired, "Yes, sir. May I help you?"

"My friend, George Baker—"

Anita looked up at the mention of George's name.

Henry asked, "Oh, how is George? We do work for his
sales company. Is he still going door to door?"

"He does love getting out and traveling. It's not my idea
of a good time."

"What do you have, son?"

Jimmy opened the wrapped bundle. "I'd like to have these title cards printed... for a moving picture I'm making."

This got Anita's attention even more. She turned to take a good look at Jimmy and averted her eyes when Jimmy saw that she was looking at him. Henry took the cards and flipped through them.

"Can do," Henry said.

"Thing is, I only have ten dollars. George says—"

Henry smiled, "Sure. George sends a lot of work our way. No problem." He gave the cards to Anita.

"Anita here will write you up."

Henry went back to his printing presses. Anita picked up a blank work order sheet, set it on the counter, and started to fill it out.

She asked, "Are you really making a moving picture?"

Jimmy leaned on an elbow on the counter and smiled, "Is that really hard to believe?"

"Do you have a name for your, um, studio?"

Thinking fast, Jimmy straightened up and paced, laying it on thick. "Oh, yes, of course, J. R. Productions. You must have heard of us. Got a spread in Culver City, some forty, fifty acres. We got a back lot that puts Universal to shame..." He could see that she was holding back a snicker, and said, "And, you're not buying any of this."

Anita shook her head in disbelief when she told him, "No, not when you only have ten dollars."

"Ouch. No, really, I am making a moving picture. Anita? By the way, I'm very pleased to meet you."

He held out his hand. She smiled and took it. She now counted the cards.

"Ten cards. Ten dollars. It shouldn't take more than three days."

"Thank you."

She placed the work order and the cards in an "In Box" on her desk, sat back down to her typewriter, and donned the headphones.

He walked backwards out of the shop while watching her. "Good-bye, Anita." He got no response, now louder. "Good-bye, Anita!" as he bumped into the door. She moved the left side of the headphones off her ear.

"Good afternoon, Mr. J. R. Productions."

"Jimmy."

"Jimmy."

She put back the headphones, turned on the Dictaphone, and resumed typing. When he was out the door, she stole a glance at him walking away and smiled.

❖ ❖ ❖

The dressing room on the *Intolerance* set was relatively quiet with only a few dressers and a few extras and actors.

Madame stood on a box while being fitted for her costume, a checkered top slung over one shoulder and a fringed skirt with wide stripes. Helen adjusted fabric and stuck pins to hold it in place.

Madame said, "Mr. Griffith says we'll be shooting my scene next week."

Helen replied, "Don't worry. I'll have your costume done by then."

"I was hoping my boys could come watch me act but it's best they stay in school."

"How old are they?"

"Nine and seven. And I have the two-year-old at a neighbor's when I'm here."

"Does your husband ever come watch?"

Suddenly, there's fire in Madame's eyes as she clenched both fists. "Don't get me riled, Helen. If I ever see that bastard again, I'll ring his neck, like I did chickens back in Louisville." Helen was surprised at her anger.

Madame stepped down from the box and paced. "As soon as the baby is born, blam! He's out the door. Coward. Just like my daddy—a preacher man who left my mother and me when I was a young'un. He didn't amount to nothin' either.

He had the Bible in one hand and all the women he could get in the other!"

Helen heard more than she wanted to but Madame continued, this time more calmly, "Sorry, Helen. I don't know what would have happened to us if Mr. Griffith hadn't shown pity and hired me."

Madame took a deep breath, and then got up back on the box to let Helen continue working on her costume. She asked, "What about you, Helen? Any chil'ens?"

Helen clutched the double locket around her neck. "Yes, no... Yes... I mean—" She turned away from Madame and wiped away a tear.

Madame stepped down, knowing that she had touched a nerve. She held Helen's hands and looked into her eyes. She said, "Dear one, if you ever you need to talk, you come to Madame."

Madame smiled. Helen nodded. Madame found a slip of paper and wrote down her address, and gave it to Helen who stuffed it into an apron pocket. In a kind voice, Madame told Helen, "And don't never believe what they say about me around here. I won't bite. Promise."

Madame smiled again and Helen smiled back. Madame then got up on the box. In her confident voice, "All right,

Helen, enough of this chatterin'. Let's get this costume finished!"

Helen regained her composure and got back to the task at hand. After finishing up with Madame, Helen walked by a table and saw an open newspaper. An advertisement caught her eye. It blindsided her. She read it, and re-read it. Near quitting time, she cleaned up her area but her mind was not on her work. The ad was for the Roxie Theater, trumpeting headliners, "Johnson and Son, First Time on the West Coast!"

CHAPTER 16

AT J. R. PRODUCTIONS

Late in the afternoon, the traffic on La Brea included an open bed truck packed with tied-down cargo. Jimmy stood in the back, hanging off a rope. When the truck stopped, Jimmy jumped off, waved "thanks" to the driver who honked and continued on his way. Jimmy then ran across the street, dodging automobiles and horse-drawn wagons, to Prospect Printing.

Inside the shop, Anita finished cleaning up her desk and picked up her coat. The overhead doorbell jangled wildly as Jimmy rushed through the door. Out of breath, Jimmy said, "Did I make it in time?"

Anita looked up at the clock. It was 4:59 p.m. "Just barely." She took a deep sigh and put her coat back on the rack.

Jimmy asked, "Are my title cards ready?"

From under the counter, Anita took out a wrapped bundle and handed it to him, and said, "They are."

Jimmy anxiously opened the bundle and flipped through the cards. He was pleased. "These are beautiful."

She smiled, "Thank you. That would be ten dollars."

He reached into a pocket and took out the ten dollar bill George gave him and handed it to her. She put the money into a cash box and made a note on the work order. "Sign here, please."

He signed the form, and said, "I'm going to film these as soon as I get home."

Filing away the work order, she asked, "Oh, how is that done?"

"I put the card in a stand and set up the camera and lights— Say, you got the time to help me?"

Picking up her coat once again, she laughed, "Not if your studio is way out in Culver City."

"No. I'm actually renting an artist studio just off Beverly, not far from here."

The temptation was too great. She wondered what she may be getting into. She also wondered what she would be missing if she didn't. She said, "All right. Give me a minute."

Jimmy smiled. He hadn't felt this much excitement in years.

Outside the shop, a streetcar stood waiting as passengers got on and off. Emerging from the shop, Anita hurried to it. She beckoned to Jimmy who was holding his package of title cards, "Come on."

Jimmy was hesitant. "It's such a nice evening. Let's walk."

She stopped. "What!? Well, how far did you say?"

"Oh, it couldn't be more than twenty, thirty blocks."

Anita was incredulous. She said, "Sorry, buster, I am not walking thirty blocks." She turned to walk in a different direction.

"Where are you going?"

She looked back at him, and said, "Home. Enjoy your walk."

Sometimes a man's got to do what a man's got to do. He told her, "All right. Streetcar it is."

Anita turned around and jumped on the streetcar. Jimmy took a deep breath and got on with her.

The streetcar, crowded with commuters, lurched when it started. In fear, Jimmy grabbed a pole and hugged it. Hemmed in by the chatter and noise of the car, Jimmy started to sweat. He smiled nervously at Anita who smiled back.

When she turned away, he closed his eyes. The chatter and noise slowly faded into the whistle and hiss of a steam engine, sounds not emanating from an electric streetcar. He was transported to a distant time and place where he now heard a little boy crying and a man's heavy footsteps. These sounds brought consternation to Jimmy's face. He forced his eyes open. The chatter and noise of the streetcar quickly returned. He suddenly realized where they were. He said, "Anita, our stop."

She nodded. When the streetcar stopped, he was the first to jump off. Anita followed.

Jimmy took a deep breath as his anxiety subsided. He pointed, and said, "My place is just around the corner." They walked toward the sidewalk in the semi-industrial area as the streetcar continued on its way.

As they walked, he continued, "Sorry, I should have told you that I don't like streetcars. They give me the willies. To me, they're like giant coffins on wheels. Do you know how many accidents they get into? And so many sick people ride these things—you can catch your death—"

He could tell that she did not believe him. He explained, "All right. I grew up on trains... and in hotel rooms. I was in vaudeville with my dad and my brother."

She stopped. "Really? Singing, dancing, telling jokes?"

"Dancing." He demonstrated by doing a short impromptu tap dance ending with flair. She gave him a small applause.

"Impressive. I was in a school play once. I didn't have the biggest part but I remember that it was fun."

They continued walking. He said, "Well, not fun for me. Really. No way for my brother and me to grow up."

A smoky, noisy automobile passed them. Jimmy pointed to it. "Now there's the future. I tell you, trains will die like the dinosaurs."

Anita asked, "So, do you walk everywhere?"

"I used to have a car but it broke down. I also had a bicycle but someone else needed it more."

"You had your own car?"

"It's somewhere in the Sierras. I had to sell it... so I could meet you." He smiled, as did she, demurely. He said, "Here we are."

Jimmy took out his keys and opened the door. They went in.

She looked around his studio and was duly impressed with the movie equipment. She said, "You weren't kidding. You really do have a movie studio here."

He pointed to the makeshift set and said, "That is where I shoot my interiors." He pointed upward, "The skylights can usually give me enough light. Do you want something to drink? I have water, beer, tea."

"How about a glass of water?" she suggested.

He went to the kitchen area, took down a glass, looked at it surreptitiously to make sure it was clean, filled it with tap water, and handed it to her. "Thank you," she said.

"My pleasure. Let me get things set up."

She watched as he set up the camera equipment and lights on his workbench to film the title cards. After filming nine cards, he placed the tenth into the card set-up.

Jimmy said, "All right, last one." He got behind the camera and started to crank it. He stopped. Jimmy told Anita, "Here. You try it."

Anita was surprised but delighted. She got behind the camera. He stood behind her and guided her hand to the crank. He was intoxicated by the nearness of her. Together they turned the crank. He then released his hand to let her keep turning.

"Whoa, girl, not so fast. Film stock is expensive." She slowed it down. "That should do it," he said. She stopped turning the crank.

He said, "I'm anxious to develop these and put them into the picture."

"Do you develop the film yourself?"

"Yes, my boss lets me use the darkroom at work."

"I can't wait to see it." She looked up at the skylight and saw the redness of the sunset on clouds. "Oh, my, it's later than I thought. I should go."

As much as he wanted her to stay, he didn't argue. "I'll walk you to the line."

He helped her into her coat.

O utside, at the streetcar stop, when the car arrived, she started to get on.

"Anita, can I call on you again?"

She turned and smiled, "Why, Mr. Johnson. You make a young girl blush." She hopped onto the streetcar and blew him a kiss. He took that for a "yes."

The streetcar left and he clapped his hands once, twirled, and headed back home. Whistling, he thought, "Life can be bad but sometimes it's not all bad."

CHAPTER 17

MADAME TELLS WHAT FOR

At the Roxie Theater, Reed and Russell were performing for the evening's audience with the piano player in accompaniment. While the packed house was enjoying them, in the back row, Helen, with a scarf over her head watched in anguish. She tried hard to enjoy the show but had to take out a handkerchief to stifle a cry.

Dancing furiously, Reed and Russell threw their canes in the air. This time, Russell caught his but Reed had to overreach. He caught it but lost his balance and fell off the stage. At first, the audience laughed, thinking it was part of the act. Helen didn't. She stood up right away, with concern on her face.

"Pop!" Russell yelled as he bounded down the side stairs to help his dad.

The piano player, seeing the commotion, realized that something was wrong. His playing tapered off, and then stopped.

Backstage, Sam was chatting with the next act ready to go on when he also realized that something was wrong. No piano, no dancing, crowd murmuring. He looked onstage. Empty. Then he saw Russell tending to Reed, and exclaimed, "What the—" Sam rushed onto the stage, then down the steps.

Helen excused her way out into the aisle and started down toward the stage. Now everyone in the audience was standing, trying to get a glimpse.

Sam and Russell picked Reed up, an arm over each of their shoulders. In pain, Reed hobbled on one foot, his back to the audience.

Russell turned his head and saw Helen approaching. Seeing him looking at her, she stopped, unsure of what to do. She turned and scurried back up the aisle. Reed didn't see her.

Turning Reed around to face the audience, Sam told them, "Don't worry, folks, he'll be all right." Reed smiled and waved to them. The audience clapped, then began to sit down.

Reed didn't even notice the woman exiting the room but Russell took one last look at her. He shook his head. Something about her seemed familiar.

Outside the theater, Helen stopped to take a breath. As she gathered herself, she realized that she was still holding her handkerchief. She stuffed it back into her purse and found a slip of paper. It was Madame's address.

❖ ❖ ❖

After work the next day, Helen, wearing her scarf around her shoulders, hailed a cab and gave the driver Madame's address. Ten minutes later the cab stopped at Madame's apartment building. For a split second, Helen thought she would tell the cab driver to take her home.

"Two dollars, ma'am," said the driver. Helen gave him the money, opened the door, and exited. Climbing a flight of stairs, Helen found Apartment 210. Again hesitant, she knocked.

A nine-year-old Negro boy answered. Nervous, Helen smiled, and then cleared her throat, "Hello. Is Madame here?" He looked at her inquisitively. Helen went on, "Nellie? Your mother?"

The nine-year-old looked inside, and called, "Mommy." Madame, holding a crying two-year-old youngster, came to the door. Looking exasperated, Madame said, "What's the bother, now?" But she brightened when she saw Helen.

"Helen! My Lord. Do come in, honey." The nine-year-old opened the door wider to allow Helen in. The living room had mismatched furniture, toys on the floor, and papers stacked haphazardly. In a corner, a three legged oak table held a hand cranked Victrola with several records leaning against the peeling wallpapered wall.

"Oh, excuse the mess. What with three boys. Come into the kitchen. I'm making a soup."

Helen had second thoughts and said, "I'm sorry. If this is a bad time—"

"Hush, child. You're here. Come in."

Her third son, a seven-year-old, ran in holding a wooden toy biplane, making flying sounds. The nine-year-old tried to take the airplane away. "Mom!"

"Hey. Hey! You two go outside. Can't you see I got company here?"

Reluctantly, the seven-year-old turned and opened the door, leading the way out with his airplane.

"Now, we can have a little peace and quiet. Helen, follow me." Madame hurried to the kitchen, turned down the flame on a large pot of soup, and stirred it. The aroma was wonderful. It made Helen think of what she might make for dinner.

The baby stopped crying. Madame put a lid on the soup pot and then set the toddler down near some wooden blocks which engaged him. Madame pointed to a kitchen chair. "Please, Helen, sit." Helen did, taking off her scarf and setting it on the table.

Madame wiped her hands on her apron and sat down. She took a deep breath. "So, Helen, what brings you out here?"

Helen started to cry, taking out her handkerchief. Madame looked concerned, put her hand on Helen's, and said, "You tell Madame all about it."

Helen apologized then said, "I... I have two sons myself—young men now—"

"I figured as much."

"Here they are when they were five and three," Helen said as she opened the locket around her neck and showed Madame the photos inside. Madame stood up to take a closer look. It was the tintype photos of Jimmy and Russell that was taken on that day at Coney Island.

Helen continued, "I haven't had any contact with either of them for over twenty years—"

Madame interrupted as she sat back in her chair, "Oh, that is not right. Why the hell why not?"

"I did something stupid a long time ago which I regret to this day."

"Damn, did you kill someone?"

Helen was taken aback, "Heavens, no!"

"Then you didn't do nothin' to keep you away from your boys. There is no way you could keep me from my sons."

"I saw my youngest, Russell, last night. He's in a vaudeville act at the Roxie Theater with his father. I wanted so much to go to him, tell him who I am, and just to... to hug him."

Madame slammed a palm to the table, startling the baby, "Hot damn! You shoulda!" Madame stood up and tried to pull Helen up. "Come on. You want us to go down there right now?"

Helen resisted, "Oh, no, no. I can't. I just can't face their father."

Madame released her and slowly sat back down. "Helen, excuse me for saying but you've got to show a little backbone."

Helen looked down and nodded.

Madame stood up and paced, "When my good-for-nothin' husband left me with three boys to raise on my own, I didn't know what the hell I was going to do. I had no family out here. I could clean houses and wash clothes but I knew acting. Then I heard this man from my own hometown in Kentucky was making moving pictures out here in Los Angeles. I went down to see him. Mr. Griffith had tears in his eyes when I told him my story. He said that I didn't have to worry about money. He hired me on the spot, first to clean up the dressing rooms, then acting. Now he pays me if I work or not. See what I mean? Show a little gumption."

She stirred the soup one more time, and then sat down. She looked at her baby playing contently, and sighed. "Without Mr. Griffith, I tell you, I couldn't feed my boys." She then asked, "What about your oldest?"

"J. J.? I don't know where he is. The act now is 'Johnson and Son.' They were a trio for the longest time—'Johnson and Sons'—but now J. J. is gone."

"You don't think that he's—" Madame swiped a finger across her throat.

Helen jerked her head back in revulsion. "Oh, no. I can't think that. I have to believe that something else happened."

Madame patted Helen's hand again. She got up, stirred the soup one more time, tasted it, and turned off the heat. She said, "Soup's on, you want to stay for dinner?"

Helen was tempted but she wrapped her scarf about her shoulders, and said, "Thank you, no. I should be going."

"Helen, I mean it. If there's anything I can do to help. I can go with you to see your son. And I'll bet you dollars to doughnuts that we'll find J. J. too."

Helen gave Madame a hug, and then turned to leave.

Madame told her, "When you see my young'uns out there, tell 'em it's dinner time. You won't have to tell 'em twice."

CHAPTER 18

INTERRUPTED ROMANCE

As Helen made her way back home, across town at Jimmy's studio, with the skylights covered, Jimmy was showing Anita his photoplay re-edited for the new title cards. She was turning the crank on the projector as he played accompaniment on his old upright piano. He said, "Wait for it."

When the final title card popped up, Jimmy exclaimed, "There— that's the card you filmed."

Anita smiled. The picture ended abruptly, leaving a white screen. Jimmy finished his playing with a flourish. Anita stopped turning the projector, and asked, "Is that the end?"

Jimmy got up and turned off the projector. "No, I have two more scenes to do. Then I'll be finished, and Sam Bixby will show it and I'll make a lot of money. I already have an idea for the next movie."

"You've got it all figured out, don't you?"

"You bet. And, when I can get a nickel ahead, I'm getting another car. No more walking or hitching."

"And no more streetcars?"

"Especially that!" They both laughed.

Anita stood up, taking Jimmy in her arms. She said, "It's all so very exciting." Then she kissed him.

Surprised at this turn of events, he kissed her lustily, rubbing his hands up and down her back. She asked, "Are you hungry?"

Jimmy with his eyes closed said, "Oh, you don't know..."

They broke apart, looking at each other. She said, "We are talking about dinner. No?"

"Yes! Definitely. Food." Jimmy would have liked a cold shower about now but headed for the kitchen area and settled for splashing cold water on his face. Drying off, he put on an apron spotted with stains from many other dinners. He looked on his shelf, and said, "I'm afraid I only have rice and beans."

"Perfect. It's what my sister and I grew up on."

Jimmy put a pan of water on his stove, then lit a match under it as Anita walked about the studio. She saw the photo of Helen below which Jimmy thumbtacked Sam's business card. Anita asked, "Who's in the photograph?"

Jimmy looked over. "Oh, that's my mother. I lost her when I was five—"

"Oh, I'm sorry."

"No, no. I mean, she's not dead, at least, I don't think she is. She mysteriously disappeared after she and Pop had a big fight. But I don't think the fight was the reason—they had lots of fights before. No, something else happened. I've been looking for her so I could find out why. Pop won't talk about it." He paused. "I don't know. In a way, I think I'm to blame—"

"Blame? How could you? Didn't you say you were five?"

"I wanted to please my father so bad. I always tried to do what he wanted, and then she left. I can't help thinking, if only I had paid more attention to her..."

Eying the poster next to the photograph, Anita asked, "This vaudeville poster—'Perry and Johnson and Their Feets of Magic.' Is 'Johnson' you?"

"No, my pop with his old vaudeville partner, Edgar Perry—"

There was a knock on the door. Jimmy looked up and wondered, "Who could that be?" He got up, went to the door, and opened it, finding Russell, wearing an overcoat.

Jimmy was happily surprised. "Russell! You found the place."

Russell answered, "Either that, or you're a damned good spittin' image of my brother."

Jimmy laughed heartily. He and Russell play punched each other, then hugged. Anita, watching this, smiled.

Jimmy ushered his brother in, "Come in, come in. Let me take your coat." He put the coat over a chair and walked to the dining table. Anita stood up.

"Anita, my little brother, Russell." Russell was taller than Jimmy. "Well, not so little. Russell, Anita." They shook hands. Russell smiled and said, "Pleased."

Jimmy asked his brother, "Had dinner yet?" as he pointed to an empty chair. "We were just sitting down to eat."

Russell sniffed the cooking smells from the stove. "Oh, your patented red beans and rice. Don't mind if I do."

Russell sat down, as did Anita. Jimmy brought over another plate and fork. "Water, beer?"

"Beer." Russell said to Anita, "It's been a long time since I've had any of Jimmy's home cookin'. Pop wasn't a very good cook, so Jimmy became our chef." She looked at Jimmy busy at the stove and smiled.

During dinner, Jimmy and Russell laughed it up while Anita was just pleased to listen.

Russell took a swig from his bottle of beer and then reminisced, "Remember that time in Jacksonville?" Jimmy just shook his head. Russell looked at Anita and said, "We were playing the Ritz Theatre, and staying at a broken down hotel.

Jimmy was sleeping and kept flicking mosquitoes off this face. Only they weren't mosquitoes. They were..."

Jimmy said, "Rats."

Anita cringed, "Oh, God."

"Big ones, too. With tails a foot long." Anita shuddered.

Russell finished the story, "I think folks as far away as Savannah heard him scream." Jimmy and Russell laughed it up some more. Jimmy said, "Oh, the joys of being on the road—I sure don't miss it."

Anita got up, and said, "I'll leave you boys to catch up."

Russell got up and said, "Please don't run off because of me."

"No, no, it's getting late. I don't want to miss the last streetcar."

Jimmy followed her and helped her with her coat. "I'll walk you."

"That's okay, Jimmy. I can find my way." At the door, she gave him a lingering kiss.

Russell reacted with a look that said, "Ooh la la." When Jimmy returned to the table, Russell reached over and punched him on a shoulder, and said, "You dirty dog."

Jimmy was dreamy-eyed, "You know, if I didn't know any better, I would say I was in love." He paused, and then asked, "You got a girl?"

Russell scoffed, "You mean, other than floozies? How can I when we're traveling all the time? Well, you know as well as I." Russell paused, and then asked, "Where have you been, man?"

"To Hell and back."

"And, now you're working at a camera shop?"

"Yeah, on Sunset Boulevard. Hey, I also learned how to fix cars. Even had a car of my own once and learned how to drive. I saw the Johnson-Jeffries fight in Reno!"

Russell shook his head in amazement, and said, "Damn, Sam."

Jimmy looked Russell in the eye, "You need to quit the act and get on with your life—"

Russell slammed his hand on the table, startling Jimmy and nearly knocking over his beer. He then stood up and paced. He said angrily, "And who would take care of Pop, dammit!? It would kill him if I left, too. I know it was hard for you to leave. Well, sonny, it's been no picnic for me. All the crap that Pop would lay on the both of us, he'd lay it on me. And I had no one to talk to, like the way we used to."

Jimmy hadn't looked at it that way. "Russell, I'm sorry. I guess I was only thinking of myself."

"You and Pop both."

"Huh?"

Russell calmed down. He sat down, looked at Jimmy, and said, "Grandpa James died."

"No!"

"Got sick this last winter, like Pop did."

"What? Pop never gets sick."

"He did this year, big time. I even had to take him to the hospital. You know, he would never go otherwise. By the grace of God, he got better. Grandpa didn't."

Now, Jimmy, feeling remorse, shook his head and said, "I wish I knew."

"No one knew where you were."

"I kept thinking I would write Grandma and Grandpa but, you know, it was one of those things you figure you'll get around to at some point."

Russell looked at Jimmy, and said, "You should write her now. She would love to hear from you."

Jimmy nodded, and then said, "How's she doing?"

"As well as can be expected. Aunt Harriet is staying with her now." Russell sighed, saying, "I would quit the act but the truth is, what would I do? Anyway, I may not have a choice. I think we are coming to the end."

"What do you mean?"

"Pop hurt himself—we can't work for a few days."

Jimmy looked concerned, "Bad?"

"Nah, just a sprained ankle. He fell off the stage the other night. I don't know how much longer he can go. He ain't no spring chicken."

Jimmy said, "His damned fool stubbornness will keep him going until he keels over on stage." Jimmy stood up, grabbed his throat, and pretended to gasp for breath. He then fell to the ground.

Russell started laughing as did Jimmy. Russell said, "He wouldn't wish for a grander finale."

Russell helped to pull Jimmy up. Jimmy started to pick up the plates from the table. Russell now realized, "Hey, don't you still owe me fifty bucks?"

Jimmy cringed, "And, I'll get it to you. As soon as I sell my picture—"

"That's right. Are you going to show me this thing or not?"

Jimmy returned from the kitchen, wiping his hands on a towel. He pointed to the sofa facing the sheet hanging off the wall that served as the screen. "Right this way, sir."

As Russell sat down, Jimmy rewound the film and re-threaded it through the projector. Russell spotted Miriam's photograph, and asked, "Still wasting your time looking for our mother?"

"Not a waste of time, man. We're getting close, really close," said Jimmy as he finished threading the film. Russell grunted his skepticism, and then asked, "Ready?"

"Yes." Jimmy turned off the lights and hand cranked the projector to start his movie.

In the hotel room where Reed and Russell were staying, Reed sat on a sofa feeling bitter. "Damned rotten luck," he thought as he looked at his propped up bandaged foot. He tried to get up and put his full weight on his bum foot, only to cringe in pain, and fell back down on the sofa. He picked up a crutch leaning on the arm of the sofa and hobbled to the bedroom.

Reed went to the top drawer of a dresser and took out a cigar box. Setting down the crutch, he sat on his bed and opened the box to reveal various mementos. He found what he was looking for—the photograph of him and his boys taken backstage the night that he threw Jimmy out. He tried to remember if it was in 1908, or 1909. He looked at the back of the photograph. "Damn," he thought, "I should have written down when this was." But in the day to day busy-ness of keeping the act together and putting food on the table, who had time for such niceties?

Staring at the photograph, he found himself weeping for his son, his first born, and whispered, "Jimmy."

To every father, his first born is extra special. It is that child that forged your parenting skills, for better or for worse. It is that first child that made you realize that you are mortal. It is that first child that you realize that you are passing on what and who you are to the next generation. In your first child, you could hold up a mirror to your own childhood, to see how you yourself grew up, how you saw your parents, how you first discovered the world.

He thought about what his mother had said at his dad's funeral, that Jimmy only did to him what he did to them. His parents didn't love him less for it. Tonight, Russell told his father that he was going to see Jimmy and invited him. Reed used his bum foot as an excuse not to go but maybe he should have.

He heard Russell unlocking the front door. He quickly put the photograph back into the cigar box and the box back into the drawer. He took out a handkerchief, wiped away any lingering tears, stood up, and hobbled back out to the living room.

"Russell, how did it go? How's Jimmy doing?"

Russell was surprised that Reed was interested. They sat down and Russell told him of Jimmy's work at the camera shop, of Jimmy learning to drive, of meeting Anita, and Jimmy's moving picture.

Reed listened attentively. He was beginning to think that perhaps he was wrong, terribly wrong about Jimmy.

Later that night, Jimmy tossed, turned, and mumbled in his sleep as he was again haunted by the recurring dream. In slow motion, silent, and sepia-toned, a steam train pulled out from a train station at first light. Five-year-old Jimmy stood at the side door of the car, looking out. He saw a woman run out frantically from the station house and toward the train. He was sure it was his mother. Reed walked up in his heavy shoes and pulled the youngster back who tried to resist but could not. Jimmy mouthed the words, "No, wait! Stop the train. Pop, make them stop the train!"

Jimmy woke up in a start, sweaty, and caught his breath. He warily went back to sleep.

CHAPTER 19

NO BREAKS

At the Sunset Camera Shop, Jimmy diligently tested a Kodak Folding Pocket camera he had just worked on, shutter still not opening. "Damn!" he thought, "Have to take it apart again—"

"Jimmy!" Callahan called in a muffled voice. He had stepped out of his windowed office with a small towel wrapped around his head. Jimmy, engrossed, didn't hear him. Callahan picked up a small bolt and tossed it onto Jimmy's workbench. Startled, Jimmy looked up.

Callahan motioned and said in a stifled voice, "Out back."

Behind the store two of Callahan's workers loaded the truck with movie film stock. Callahan handed Jimmy two purchase orders. He talked haltingly. "Deliver thish... film stock. I can't."

Jimmy asked, "You got a toothache?"

Callahan replied sarcastically, "No, boy, I like wearing a towel over my head. Yesh! I'm going to see the damned dentish."

"Okay, okay!" Jimmy said as he cranked over the engine and then got in behind the wheel. He looked at the purchase orders as Callahan gave him instructions, "First, to the Lincoln Motion Picture Company and then to... the Mack Sennett Studios. Sennett needs thish by 3 o'clock sharp... No later..."

"Got it, Boss."

Callahan turned to walk away, holding his painful jaw. One last admonishment, "Don't mesh up. Sennett is my big-gesh account."

As Jimmy started the truck, he said, "Don't worry, Mr. Callahan, what can go wrong?"

Jimmy arrived at the offices of the Lincoln Motion Picture Company, housed in a small non-descript building. The brakes squealed as the truck stopped. Jimmy thought, "Hmm, there's a new sound. Gotta tell the boss." Jimmy got out of the truck, picked up two canisters of film stock from the back, and went in.

The Lincoln Motion Picture Company had been formed earlier in the year as one of the first black filmmaking companies. The driving force behind the company was a Negro actor named Noble Johnson. Noble was a contract player with

Universal Studio but wanted to make non-comedies with a colored cast and colored sensibilities, something that Hollywood at the time was unable or unwilling to do; the same idea that Jimmy had hit upon independently. Noble, with his strong physique (6 foot 2 inches, 215 pounds) and lighter-toned skin, was able to portray a number of different ethnic minorities, including Native American, Latino, Middle Eastern. He was in high demand. Currently, the company was making its first film, *The Realization of a Negro's Ambition*, the story of a Negro man trying to break into the white dominated oil industry.

Inside the building, Jimmy walked in to see a secretary. She looked up and smiled.

Looking at the purchase order, Jimmy said, "Hi. Film stock delivery for, uh, Noble Johnson."

"Oh, you just missed them. They went out on location at Signal Hill."

Jimmy looked quizzically, "Where's that?"

"Down near Long Beach."

"Damn. That's pretty far. Can I just leave these here?"

"You could but they might need them." She wrote down directions. "Here's where they are."

"Well, I have to be back in town by 3." He looked at the wall clock. It was only 10:30. Jimmy took the directions and said, "I guess I have time."

The secretary smiled and said, "I suspect you do, darlin'."

Jimmy smiled back as he walked out with the canisters and put them back into the truck.

Among the many pumping oil wells, a small film crew was shooting a scene when Jimmy drove up and stopped, brakes squealing even louder. Dust from the truck tires enveloped the actors and crew, much to their chagrin, coughing, and slapping the dust away.

"What the hell?" one of the actors asked.

Jimmy got out of the truck. Taking out the film stock, he hailed, "Noble Johnson?"

Noble, wearing an oil rig helmet turned his attention to Jimmy. Handsome, charismatic, he was like the James Earl Jones of his day. "I'm Noble Johnson."

"Film stock delivery."

"Give them to Harry."

Harry Gant, the cameraman, the only white person among the crew and actors, took the canisters. Jimmy gave Noble the purchase order which he signed. Noble asked, "Have trouble finding us?"

"A couple of wrong turns but I'm here."

"You could have just left the film at the office. We have enough." Jimmy clenched in disbelief. Noble continued, "Well, we're on a tight schedule. Again, thanks. Harry, ready?"

"Ready."

"Let's do it." The cast and crew got into their positions.

Jimmy asked, "Mr. Johnson, since I came out all this way, do you mind if I stay a bit to watch?"

"Be my guest. Clarence?"

Clarence Brooks was a financial partner in the company and an actor in this production. He offered Jimmy a folding chair.

Jimmy became so engrossed with the production that he forgot the time. Later, in the afternoon, he helped the crew pack up their equipment. He turned to Noble, and said, "Thanks, Mr. Johnson. I learned a lot watching you guys. I'm making my own—" Suddenly, it dawned on him. "Oh, shit. What time is it?"

Noble looked at his watch. "Two-thirty."

"Dammit, I gotta go. I have to be back in Hollywood by 3."

"You best hurry."

Jimmy jumped up and ran to his truck. Noble and crew watched Jimmy speed off, dust flying. Harry asked, "What in Sam Hill was that?" They chuckled, shaking their heads.

J immy drove like a maniac, weaving in and out of traffic, crossing dangerously into the other lane around slower trucks. Mostly just two lane roads, some unpaved. Other cars honked at his rudeness.

Entering the hills of Hollywood, Jimmy went down a steep incline. As he tried to slow down, the brakes started smoking. He looked out the window at his wheels.

Meanwhile, at the famous Mack Sennett Studios on Glendale Boulevard, much activity was going on. While there was filming on studio stages, on a nearby street, a film crew was shooting a scene with the Keystone Kops. The street was roped off to keep back spectators who lined the sidewalks.

Inside a darkened projection room at the studio, a projectionist had just finished showing the latest comedy opus. Someone flipped on the lights. Mack Sennett, no jacket, suspendered trousers, got up. A few other people, including Sid, the director, remain seated. Sid looked nervous.

Sennett said, "You know, Sid. I'm not laughing. I was squirming. I should be laughing. I've seen better film—"

Others in the room repeated in unison, "—in a bowl of chicken soup."

Sid tried to defend himself, "But, Mr. Sennett—"

"It needs—and how I thought of this—another chase."

Sid rolled his eyes.

Meanwhile Jimmy closed in on the studio. His brakes were shot. He came around the corner, screeching. Jimmy saw the Keystone Kops film crew ahead. His foot pumped the brakes but to no avail. He thought, "No, no, no!"

He stuck his head out the window and honked his horn repeatedly. He yelled, "Get out of the way!!"

Jimmy crashed through the street barrier. The Kops and crew scattered as Jimmy's truck raced through them and the scene. The Kops gathered themselves, and then chased him.

Trying to slow down, Jimmy turned corners, went up one street, down another, with the Kops chasing, whistles blowing, billy clubs waving.

Turning down another street, Jimmy saw a fruit vendor pushing his large cart of fresh fruit while crossing the street. Jimmy banged on his horn repeatedly. The man saw what was coming but was unsure of what to do. At the last minute, he jumped out of the way as Jimmy plowed into his cart, scattering fruit, notably bananas. The Kops, still in chase, ran through, slipping on the peels.

Jimmy screeched around another corner and managed to find the main gate of the studio, and drove in. He was heading toward the projection room building with no place to turn. Jimmy pulled extra hard on the emergency brake. The brake handle broke and pulled off the floor. He looked at it in disbelief, and then tossed it out the window. Jimmy honked his horn repeatedly, closed his eyes, and braced for impact.

Inside the projection room, a harried assistant opened the door as Sennett was opening the blinds. The assistant said, "Mr. Sennett, where's that film stock? We got people just standing around!"

Sennett looked out the window, heard the honking, and saw the truck heading towards them. He said, "I think it's here— Oh, shit. Look out, everyone! He's not going to stop!"

All in the room hustled to the opposite wall, knocking over chairs.

The truck slammed into the building, breaking a window, but finally stopping. Steam rose from a broken radiator. The Kops converged. Sennett and the others ran out. Jimmy got out of the truck hastily.

In a shaky voice, Jimmy said, "Mr. Sennett. Your film stock is here."

Sennett pointed to the truck smashed into the building. To his director, Sennett said, "Now, that's funny!" Realizing the gravity of the moment, Sennett asked Jimmy, "You okay, kid?"

Jimmy checked body and limb and found no blood or broken bones. He then fell to the ground in a faint.

Back at Sunset Camera, a tow truck unhitched Callahan's mangled truck out in front of the shop. Looking dejected, Jimmy came out the front door with a small wooden box of his personal belongings and walked away. From inside the store, a fuming Callahan shook an angry fist at Jimmy and put a "Help Wanted" sign in the window.

The rude clerk, the one that never got along with Jimmy, stood at the window. Sarcastically, he smiled and waved "bye-bye." Callahan slapped him on the back of his head and told him to get back to work.

CHAPTER 20

A CHANGE OF HEART

At the Roxie Theater, Reed, using his cane, walked fairly sprightly with Russell past a long line of people waiting to buy tickets. Reed whistled in amazement, "Look at this line. Good God, who does Sam have headlining?" Russell shrugged.

They walked into Sam's office where Sam was working a manual calculator and writing down figures. Sam looked up and said, "Gentlemen. Reed, how's the foot?"

Reed bounced on his "bum" foot. "I should be back in business in a couple of days."

"We've missed you two here."

"Hey, who are you headlining out there? I've never seen such a crowd outside."

"Charlie Chaplin."

"Who? Never heard of the guy. Has he been playing in vaudeville long?"

Sam thought for a moment, "Well, maybe back in England."

"Huh?"

Russell informed his dad, "Pop. Chaplin's a moving picture actor!"

"Damn! You mean all those people are waiting to see a moving picture?"

Sam pointed to his ledger book, and said, "You bet. It's helping my bottom line. Jimmy is damned smart to get into the business."

Reed was mildly surprised by this, "Really?"

Sam picked up two tickets off his desk and said, "Hey, why don't you two stay and watch the show? On me."

Russell's face lit up while Reed shook his head, and said, "Wish we had the time."

Russell said, "Are you joking? Right now, all we got is time." He grabbed the tickets and ushered his dad out. "Thanks, Sam."

Sam went back to his calculator, and said, "Enjoy."

In the theater, movie goers, including Russell and Reed, found their seats. Though this was not Russell's first sit-down movie experience, Russell was excited to be watching this flicker with his dad. On the Circuit, when Reed caught a nap in the afternoons, Russell would go out and find entertainment for himself. Sometimes he watched white vaudeville shows to see what they were like. In addition to similar song and dance acts, he saw dogs jumping through hoops, a man throwing knives at a pretty girl who tried hard not to look scared, and even a guy in funny clothes and a goatee reciting Shakespeare, whoever he was. Or, he might take in a burlesque show, like Madame Rentz' Female Minstrels, but more often than not he'd watch a moving picture. He began imagining life after vaudeville. Could he too be an actor in the movies? That possibility was why he found Jimmy's foray into movie making especially fascinating.

He was also a little jealous that Jimmy had found a girlfriend. The women who traveled in the Circuit did not really suit him. Reed found Miriam but look how that turned out. Still, he knew of many happily married couples in vaudeville, like his mother's parents, so it was possible.

Although Reed couldn't care less about watching a motion picture, he was impressed with the nearly full attendance in the house as he looked about. The lights went down. The audience reacted with anticipation. The piano player started to play music.

Sam had billed the Charlie Chaplin film, *The Fireman*. The audience, including Russell, laughed it up. Reed tried hard not to enjoy it, even trying to avert his eyes. Finally, he couldn't help it. The laughter was contagious. Slowly, he looked at the screen, started to smile, then chuckled, then with Russell and the others laughed out loud.

❖ ❖ ❖

After the movie, Russell and Reed walked back to their hotel. They passed by stores, diners, taverns, and a barber shop. Reed stopped and looked in the front door at the many customers chatting with the barbers. It brought back memories of his father's shop.

Russell asked, "What is it, Pop?"

Reed shook his head, and muttered, "Nothin'," as they continued walking back to their hotel.

Reed had to admit, "Looks like that Chaplin fellow could have a future. But I wonder if he could hold a candle to us on stage."

Russell could only laugh, "Oh, Pop."

Reed offered, "I ain't saying I'm wrong but maybe Jimmy is on to something with this moving picture business."

Russell stopped, pondering this change in attitude. Reed continued walking. Russell smiled, and then caught up. He said, "You know, Pop, maybe he is. Just maybe he is."

They walked past an especially noisy tavern, the Nite Owl. Inside, lots of customers, men and women, were drinking and smoking amid loud piano music. Edgar Perry, unshaven, in ragged clothes, danced to the music. Down but not out, he put on a good show. Wilson, the tavern owner, tolerated him because he drew in extra customers, especially more women. However, he wasn't averse to throwing Edgar out if he caused any trouble.

When the music stopped, Edgar finished with a flourish. Appreciative patrons applauded and tossed coins his way. He greedily fell on his knees and picked up his treasure.

A customer wanted more and pleaded, "Give us another, Edgar."

Edgar was thankful and replied, "In ten minutes, ladies and gents." He bowed, and then headed for the bar.

A woman customer offered to her date, "He's good."

Her date replied, "Yeah, they say he used to be famous."

Edgar squeezed himself among the other patrons at the bar. Counting his coins, he ordered, "Wilson, my man. The usual, and this time, make it a double." He grinned, revealing the missing front tooth.

Wilson poured him his drink. Edgar quickly downed it and slapped the glass down on the bar, demanding another. The bartender did what he does best. As Edgar drank, he couldn't help but overhear two men at the bar next to him.

The first man said, "I thought you and the missus were going out tonight."

"We were going to the Roxie to see Reed Johnson dance, him and his son."

The second man said, "Hot damn. Is he still around?"

The first man replied, "Yeah, first time out here. Better go before he heads back East."

Edgar, suddenly seized by rage, slowly set down his glass. He turned around and started walking out of the bar.

A customer yelled out, "Hey, Edgar, how about another?"

Edgar angrily said to the man, "Piss off!"

The customer grumbled and the crowd murmured. Wilson raised an eyebrow when saw that Edgar had left a half-finished drink on the bar.

CHAPTER 21

A DEVASTATING DEAD END

Jimmy sat at the table in his studio feverishly writing on a piece of paper. Blake and Rose, in costume, were standing on the set, impatiently waiting for the scene to start.

Blake said, "Come on, Jimmy, you said you finally figured out the ending." He looked at his pocket watch and said, "We don't have all day."

Jimmy looked up, his eyes a little wild, and said, "All right. All right." He got up and said, "Let's try this one." He showed them the revised scene. They read what he wrote, mouthed the dialogue that wouldn't be heard, and made exaggerated gestures in rehearsal. Rose and Blake nodded to each other. Blake said, "Okay, Jimmy, we got it."

Jimmy got behind the camera and started cranking it. He said, "All right. Start."

Blake and Rose got into position and began the scene just as Jimmy had written it. Suddenly, Jimmy stopped the camera, and said, "No, wait. It doesn't work."

"What? The camera again?"

"No, what I just wrote." Blake and Rose cringed in frustration. Jimmy grabbed the paper and sat back down. He concentrated hard, crossed out lines, wrote new lines while mumbling to himself. Blake started to gather his things. He turned to Rose, and said, "Come on, sweetie, we got to go."

Jimmy looked up, and said, "Huh?" He put his pencil down, resigned that the day was a bust. He said, "Okay. Sorry. I'll get this ending polished. How about Saturday?"

Blake tried to find the words, and said, "Um. That's the thing, Jimmy. We won't be here Saturday. We're gone tomorrow. Remember, we're headed back East."

Shocked, Jimmy exclaimed, "What!?"

Blake said, "I thought I told you." He looked at Rose. "Didn't I tell him, darling?"

Rose said sweetly, "You did, sugar." She looked at Jimmy, and said, "We're moving to Philadelphia."

Jimmy was adamant, "No, no, you can't. I guess I didn't hear. Then, you have to do this. Today! Please."

Blake pointed to the paper on the table that Jimmy was struggling with, and said, "We'd like to oblige but you don't have the ending. Listen, we're damned disappointed too. We were hoping this could be a jump start for us as well."

Rose said, "This has been a valuable experience for us all."

Gathering their things, Blake said, "After we're settled, if you want to pay for our trip back, we'll be happy to finish your picture. Good luck."

Rose took Jimmy's hand, and then kissed him on the cheek.

Jimmy stood in shock as Blake and Rose walked out. Jimmy ran to the doorway as Rose got into their car. He reminded them, "But we signed a contract."

Blake started the car, and then got in. Driving off, he laughed and said, "So, sue us."

This irked Jimmy to no end. He slowly walked back into his studio. He angrily crumbled up the scene he was writing and tossed it against the wall near the tintype of his mother. He went to the photo and screamed at it, "How can I finish this damned thing when I don't know why a mother would leave her sons? Why!?"

He suddenly had an idea. "Wait. That's it." He picked up the crumbled paper that he just threw, flattened it out, and re-read it. He frantically re-wrote more lines. He read it over and beamed, "Hey, I got it. I got it!"

He ran out of his studio and saw Blake and Rose in the distance. He yelled, "Blake, Rose, I got it! Come back!" He yelled louder, "Come back!!"

They didn't hear him. In a softer voice, he kept repeating, "Come back, come back..." Dejected, he turned and slowly walked back inside, dropping the paper on the ground outside. A breeze fluttered it down the street. He closed the door.

Inside, he let out an anguished scream. Sitting down, breathing hard, he pondered his next move. There went his dreams of finishing his photoplay soon, of selling it to Sam Bixby, of paying back his brother, and of proving to his father that he was not the failure that Reed thought he was. He slammed his fist down on the table.

Many thoughts raced through his head when he heard a car pull up outside and stop. He heard a knock on the door. He looked up, momentarily delighted. "They're back! Thank God." He jumped up and rushed to swing open the door. "You've come back—" Only it wasn't Blake and Rose. It was George. George had news that caused Jimmy to whoop, jump in the air, and hug him.

O n La Brea, George drove up in his Lambert, top down, and parked in front of Prospect Printing. Jimmy, wearing a suit jacket and tie, sat in the front passenger seat. He jumped out with a bouquet of flowers, and rushed into the shop.

It was quitting time. Inside, Anita got on her coat just as Jimmy barged in. She was pleasantly surprised.

"Jimmy, my, aren't we all dressed up. What's the occasion?" She saw the flowers and made the wrong assumption. She said, "Why, those are lovely. For me?"

Jimmy realized his mistake. "Oh, sorry, these... actually... aren't for you."

Anita's a bit disappointed, and joked, "Oh, for your new girlfriend?"

"No. They're for my mother!"

"What!"

"I'm going to see her right now. Come with me?"

"We're not going to walk, are we?"

"No, baby, this time, we're going first class."

Jimmy and Anita stepped out of the shop and towards George's car. Anita slowed down when she saw the car and who was driving.

She remembered when she first met George. It happened about a year before. George had come into the shop with work from his company. They struck up a conversation. George was a charmer, a big reason he was such a successful salesman. After much persistence, Anita went out with George, then again, and again. At first, she enjoyed his company, riding in his car. She didn't really know anyone who had an automobile. It made her feel special. She was the envy of her girlfriends. But soon things started to go sour. With his work, he would be out of town for long stretches. That wasn't his fault, she knew. But when he came back from one such trip, she had the feeling that he was losing interest. She could tell that he wasn't in the relationship for the long haul. Then she saw him tooling about town in his car with two other young women wearing feathered hats. She confronted him. They had a nasty argument. She broke off their relationship. George was not unhappy about it. All of these thoughts flashed in her mind when she saw George again.

Jimmy, unaware of their prior relationship, gave introductions, "George, this is Anita."

George was grim, "Yes. I know Anita." Trying to be gracious, he said to her, "Hello."

Jimmy surmised, "Oh, right. Henry does work for your company." He couldn't see the coldness between them.

She said curtly, "Hello, George. How are you?"

He opened his mouth to answer but before he could utter a word, she said, "I'll get in the back." She did, on the passenger side. Jimmy got in the front, happy and oblivious. He stood up, looking forward to reacquainting with his mother. He said, "Wagons, ho!"

When George accelerated out of the parking space, Jimmy fell back down into his seat, surprised and laughing.

In the dressing room barn, Helen and other dressers were frantically putting the final costumes on extras for Griffith's next scene. The extras then ran out, allowing Helen, Sophie, Doris, and the other dressers a little respite.

On West Sunset Boulevard, George's car approached Griffith's studio. He had to stop the car to allow the dozen or so extras to make their way across the street to the Babylonian set.

Jimmy asked, "Are we here?"

George said, "No, this is where Griffith is making his new moving picture."

Jimmy exclaimed, "Griffith? D. W. Griffith?"

As George continued on his way, Jimmy marveled at the blocks long set and said, "Damn, look at this thing."

As they got to the front of the set, Anita saw Griffith in a straw hat in the basket of the tethered balloon directing through a megaphone in a loud voice. She pointed, "Look, that must be him up there!"

Jimmy looked up, saw his adversary, and said, "There's that bastard." Incensed, he again stood up, holding onto the windshield, and yelled at the famed director, "Hey, Griffith, making another hateful picture? You son of a bitch—"

Griffith was focused on his work, giving direction to the hundreds of extras before him. However, he was momentarily distracted by Jimmy's nearly inaudible tirade. He looked down on the street and saw George's car driving past with Jimmy standing, shaking a fist at him.

In the car, George was laughing. Jimmy still had words, "Yeah, come down here, sucker. I'll show you—"

George pulled Jimmy down into his seat who started laughing too. Even Anita was amused.

O minous gray clouds covered the sky as George drove slowly in a quiet and modest neighborhood. Checking addresses against that written on a piece of paper, George stopped at a well groomed cottage with a white picket fence.

George said, "Here we are, Jimmy, the home of Miriam Johnson. Want me to go in with you?"

Jimmy took a deep breath, and said, "No, let me do this." He held out his right hand, slightly shaking. "Look at me, a man who has no stage fright."

Anita leaned over and gave Jimmy a lingering kiss on the cheek, while looking at George slyly. George rolled his eyes. Jimmy got out of the car with the flowers and walked through the front gate.

On the front porch of the cottage, Jimmy knocked on the screen door. A colored woman, looking about the right age as his mother, opened her door, and asked, "Yes?"

With his heart racing, Jimmy inquired, "Pardon me, but are you... Miriam Johnson?"

She answered quizzically, "I am."

This woman did not look anything like the tintype of his mother but Jimmy was not thinking about that.

"Mom?"

"Excuse me?"

"It's me, Jimmy... J. J."

Miriam was taken aback. She said, "I'm sorry. I don't know you. I don't know any Jimmy. You are mistaken—"

"Miriam Johnson? From Seattle?"

"Yes, but—"

"You have another son, Russell, and a husband, Reed."

"No, I don't. That's wrong. My husband was Earl but he passed away—"

He took out the tintype of his mother and showed it to her. Jimmy sounded desperate as he demanded, "Isn't this you? Taken at Coney Island?"

She looked and shook her head. Alarmed, she said, "I've never been to Coney Island! I don't know what you're talking about. Good-bye." She tried to slam the door but Jimmy stuck his foot in it.

In the car, George and Anita were having terse words. Anita said, "George, forget it. I'm not going to relive the past—"

They heard Miriam scream. George looked up, and muttered, "Oh, shit." He stood up, stepped on the passenger seat, jumped out of his car, and raced through the front gate.

At the porch, Jimmy hit the flowers against his leg in frustration. He said, "This can't be happening. You have two sons, Jimmy and Russell—"

Miriam was still trying to close the door and was frightened, "No, no. Go away!"

George arrived at the porch and understood what was happening. He said, "Jimmy. Jimmy! Stop!"

George took Jimmy by the shoulders and pulled him away from the door. He looked at Miriam, and said, "Sorry, ma'am, our apologies. We must have the wrong address."

Miriam pointed an angry finger at Jimmy, and said, "Keep that nut away from me. I have a telephone in here now. I can call the police."

George said, "No need for that. We're leaving."

She closed and double locked the door. Broken flowers were strewn on her porch.

George led Jimmy away. At the car, an angry Jimmy tossed the remaining bouquet on the sidewalk as he and George got back in. Anita looked concerned, and asked, "What happened?"

Jimmy said through clenched teeth more to himself than to either in the car, "She said she was Miriam Johnson, from Seattle. But she didn't know me."

George replied, "What can I say, man? She was the wrong Miriam Johnson. I have to apologize."

Anita leaned toward Jimmy. Trying to be helpful, she said softly, "Jimmy, I am so sorry—"

Jimmy, frustrated and unreasonable, turned to her, "What do you know about it? Huh!? You're lucky. You still have your family."

George tried to defend Anita, and said, "Hey! Leave her mother and sister out of it. Anita was only trying to help—"

"Wait. How do you know about her mother and sister?" It finally dawned on him as he surmised, "Oh... Of course you know her. I'm such an idiot."

Jimmy got out of the car, slammed the door, and turned to walk away.

Anita beckoned, "Come back, Jimmy. What George and I had is no more."

George said, "She's right, Jimmy! Get back into the car."

Jimmy continued walking.

George started the car. Anita said, "George, you're not just going to leave him!" George honked his horn at Jimmy and crept the car towards him. Without looking back, Jimmy waved them to leave him.

George said, "Anita, you don't know him like I do. When he gets this way, it's best to let him be." George turned the car around and slowly drove away. Anita looked back at Jimmy confused, not understanding him. She sat back down, tearing up, pondering their relationship.

That night, rain drizzled down on Jimmy as he reached his studio. Soaking wet, he took out his keys and walked in. He lit a fire in the wood stove, got undressed and into some dry clothes. Shivering, he sneezed as he hung his wet clothes on a line near the stove.

He filled a tea kettle with water and set it on the stove. Exhausted by the emotional roller coaster of the day and the long walk home, he got into bed, pulled the covers up and immediately fell asleep. Awakened by the loud whistling tea kettle, he made himself get up. Sipping the tea to warm himself up, he, like Anita, had a lot to ponder.

NO FUTURE

J immy woke up feeling disconnected to the world. He tried to make a fresh pot of coffee but realized that he had just run out of coffee. He decided to re-use the coffee grounds from the morning before. His landlord had come by three days before wanting the rent. Jimmy promised he would get it. After the landlord left, Jimmy went to his bed and lifted the mattress. In a sock, he fished out two dollars. He reached into his pockets and found only a few coins, the key to his studio, and his mother's photo. He sighed, and placed the photo face down on his dresser. Fired from Sunset Camera the week before, Jimmy realized that he must find another job.

Not only did he need money to pay the rent and buy food but because he lost his use of the darkroom at Sunset Camera, he needed money to develop his film on his own. Even if he wanted to crowd a makeshift darkroom into his bathroom, darkroom chemicals did not come cheap. He could send it out for developing but that wasn't cheap either. And, of course, all of this was moot since his actors moved away.

The first place he went to in his job quest was the Lincoln Motion Picture Company. He felt a kinship with Noble and company. When he walked in, the secretary looked up and smiled. "Well, hello, again. Got another delivery for us?"

Jimmy shook at the thought and clenched his teeth. If he had just dropped off the film stock at the office in the first place on that day, he wouldn't have driven all the way to Kingdom Come and back, wouldn't have crashed Callahan's truck, and wouldn't have lost his job. He was on a different mission now and tried to be civil.

"Uh, no, not this time. Could I have a word with Noble Johnson?"

"He's having a meeting with his partners. Would you like to wait?"

Having no choice, he said, "Yes." He looked around and sat on a chair. He gave the secretary a crooked smile. She smiled back and asked, "Would you like a cup of coffee?"

Remembering the weak cup he had that morning, he said, "Love to." She went into a back room and came out with a cup of coffee. "Cream or sugar?"

He shook his head, "No, thank you." She brought it and he savored the strong brew as he picked up a copy of *The Los Angeles Examiner* on the table next to him.

I nside an office, Noble, Clarence, and two other partners, all in business suits, sat at a table with papers in front of them. A book was in front of Clarence.

Noble said, "We can get distribution for *Ambition* through my brother in Omaha." The other two nodded in agreement. "Any new business?"

Clarence pushed the book to Noble. "This is the book I told you about by this fellow, Oscar Micheaux."

Noble picked it up, opened it to the title page, and said, "Oh, yes, *The Homesteader*."

Clarence continued, "The story is about a Negro man making his way in South Dakota. It could be a future project, maybe after *Trooper*."

Noble leafed through it. "I'll read it. Contact Mr. Micheaux and see if we can come to terms." Clarence made a note. "Any other business?" The other two shook their heads. "Then, meeting adjourned." Noble looked at his pocket watch. "I've got to get back to Universal."

The secretary heard the partners leaving their meeting room. She said, "Someone here to see you, Noble."

Noble looked at Jimmy and smiled, "You're Sunset Camera. Never forget a face."

Jimmy leaped up and hurled himself at Noble with his hand outstretched, "Yes, sir. Jimmy Johnson." Shaking Noble's hand, Jimmy said, "Only, um, I lost my job that day."

"Oh, very sorry to hear that. I hope it wasn't because of us?"

Diplomatically, Jimmy said, "No."

"Then, what can I do for you?" Noble said.

"I was wondering if you had any work for me here. Anything. I could sweep, haul equipment..." The words caught in his throat as he said, "Drive a truck."

Noble looked at his partners, and said, "Hey, do we have any job openings for an enterprising young man?" The partners grimaced and shook their heads.

"I wish we did, Jimmy—"

"I even know a thing or two about film production. I can edit—"

Noble was impressed but said, "We have an editor. We are just finishing our first production. If we had anything left in the budget... Maybe in a year—"

Jimmy pleaded, "You know, I'm a Johnson. You're a Johnson. We must be related somewhere. You mean you can't do for family?"

Noble smiled and took Jimmy by the shoulders. "Look, kid. I like you but I'm telling you. We got nothing."

Noble released Jimmy and reached for a pen and paper and started writing. "I want you to visit Madame—"

Jimmy stood firmly and said, "Hey, no, I don't need a madame. I have a girlfriend... I think. Anyway, I can get girlfriends!"

"No, no, not that kind of madame. This is an acquaintance of mine, Madame Sul-te-wan, a motion picture actress. She can probably get you into a picture. Mention my name."

Jimmy couldn't believe his ears. "Really? That's great!" He grabbed the address.

Noble continued, "And I have some connections at Universal. I'll ask around."

Jimmy shook Noble's hand vigorously and said, "That would be swell." He held up Madame's address. "I'll talk to her right away."

Jimmy flew out the door. Noble smiled as he looked at his partners. He said, "Remember when we were all so idealistic?"

His partners nodded wistfully.

At Prospect Printing, Anita was typing when she looked up and saw Jimmy coming across the street. Still hurting from their last encounter, she did not want to see him right now. She got up and went through back door just as Jimmy walked in. He caught a glimpse of her.

"Anita..."

She closed the back door pretending not to hear him. Jimmy went back behind the counter and knocked on the door. Henry came out, closing the door behind him.

Henry said, "Can I help you?"

"Anita. I need to talk with Anita."

"She's not here."

"But, I just saw her—"

"You're mistaken."

"But..."

"Son, I did you a favor once. Do me a favor, and just leave. I don't want any trouble."

Jimmy nodded that he understood. At first hesitating, he now realized that he blew it with her and sadly left the shop. Anita peeked around the door and saw him walking away. She wondered why she seemed to have so much trouble with men. She also wondered, with Jimmy, what might have been.

CHAPTER 23

DIGGING OUT
OF A HOLE

At Madame's apartment building, Helen, wearing a flow-ered dress, walked out and turned to her right. Jimmy walked in from the opposite direction, not noticing her, as he checked for Madame's address. Finding the building, he walked in as Helen continued on her way a half a block away.

Inside her apartment, Madame was whistling as she cleaned the kitchen table. She noticed a scarf on the counter, and said, "Helen."

She grabbed the scarf and rushed to the front door. She un-locked, and then swung it open to find Jimmy standing there ready to knock. Both were startled.

Catching her breath, Madame patted her heart, and said, "Damn. You scared the bejesus out of me."

Jimmy asked, "Sorry but are you Madame Sul-te-wan?"

She answered, "I am, and you be..."

"Jimmy Johnson."

She suddenly remembered the scarf. Talking swiftly, she said, "Listen, Jimmy. A lady just left here—Helen—wearing a flowered dress. Old enough to be your mother. She forgot her scarf. Can you catch her?" She handed him the scarf. He was momentarily bewildered.

Urgently, she said, "Go, go! What's the matter, you got glue on your shoes?" She pushed him. Jimmy turned and lurched down the stairs.

Outside, he looked one way, then the other. There was no one in sight.

Madame heard Jimmy's footsteps coming up the stairs. She was still in her doorway when Jimmy returned with the scarf. He handed it back to her, and said, "Didn't see anyone."

She took back the scarf and said, "Oh, well. Thanks for doing that. Now, Jimmy, what can I do you for?"

Jimmy said, "Noble Johnson of the Lincoln Motion Picture Company told me to look you up."

"Oh, yes... Noble."

"I'm looking for a job. He said that you might have some motion picture work."

Madame sized him up. "Maybe. What can you do?"

"Anything. I can sweep, drive, operate a camera, edit film. I can dance, act. I've been in vaudeville—"

"Hell's Bells, me too! Heard of the Three Black Cloaks? I was Creole Nell."

He's never heard of them or her but said, "Yes, of course."

"Well, I know they're always looking for more extras in the picture I'm in. Pays five dollars per day."

This got Jimmy excited, "That's great! I can be an extra!"

Madame said, "I'm working for Mr. D. W. Griffith—"

A bombshell. Jimmy said, "Hold it, hold it! Did you say, D. W. Griffith?"

"Yes."

"Sorry, but there is no way in Hell I can work for him. Not since *The Birth of a Nation*."

"I was in that picture."

"You were?"

"Yeah, I was the one who spit on the ground in front of Dr. Cameron."

Jimmy wracked his memory of that scene. He said, "That was you?" He now saw the resemblance. "Yeah, that was you."

"Mr. Griffith wrote a bigger scene for me. I got to wear the finest gown and jewelry but the damned censors cut it out."

"No, no. I can't work for Griffith. Don't you have anything else?"

"I don't."

"Well, I'd rather dig ditches."

"Somebody's got to. Good afternoon, Jimmy." She swung the door closed just inches from his nose. Then he turned and left, thinking, "Man, that was rude. She and Griffith deserve one other."

A bit later, while Madame was cleaning up her kitchen, she heard a knock on the door. Thinking it was Jimmy, she slammed down her cleaning rag and muttered to herself, "Oh, what does he want now?"

She unlocked, and then swung opened the door. It was Helen who said, "Silly me, I forgot my scarf." Madame smiled as she went to retrieve it.

Jimmy spent the next few days looking for work at other studios. No luck. He checked with Noble about work at Universal. None. He inquired at other camera shops, other fix-it shops, garages. Nothing. Reluctantly, he found himself at City Hall, at the Public Works Department.

The next day he was digging ditches with a pick axe. He was with a dozen other workers, toiling in the brutal August sun that was part of summer in the City of Angels. The other workers were brawny, shirtless, and sweating. Jimmy seemed out of place with his skinny body. He was not used to this grinding manual labor. He stopped, leaned on his pick, and wiped his brow with a handkerchief.

A foreman wearing a fedora saw him and barked, "Hey, keep digging. We don't pay you to watch."

Jimmy quickly lifted up his pick and swung it into the ground, mumbling obscenities under his breath.

Finally, at the end of the day, it was quitting time. This couldn't have come any sooner for Jimmy. Each worker stood in line for his daily pay. The paymaster dropped Jimmy's pay, in coins, into his left hand. His right hand was wrapped in his handkerchief. Jimmy looked askance at the meager amount.

The paymaster was anxious to get his job done and go home. He growled at Jimmy, "Move on." Jimmy reluctantly did so.

That evening, Jimmy walked into his studio, feeling worse than when he had left that morning. He went to a shelf and took down a jar of salve, a first aid kit, and some hydrogen peroxide. He sat down and awkwardly opened the jar with his left hand while holding the jar under his right arm. He opened the handkerchief wrapped around his hand to reveal open blisters on his palms. He almost let out a scream as he poured the peroxide over the wound and then applied the salve. From the first aid kit, he re-wrapped his injured hand with clean gauze, tying it off with his teeth.

Later that evening, Jimmy had a sandwich and crackers for dinner since it was too hard for him to open a can or to cook with his bum hand. He did manage to open his last bottle of beer by holding the bottle between his knees. He sat at his 80 key piano, staring off in space. He absent-mindedly played with his left hand just two keys over and over again while deep in thought. Could his life get any worse? Two weeks ago, he was flying high. Now, he had lost his job, his actors, his girlfriend. And another dead end to finding his mother. He thought, "It never pays to think that life is going well. As soon as you think it, then BAM, something will come up and bite you in the ass." He finished his beer, sighed, got up, turned off the lights, and crawled into bed, his body aching for rest. He fell into a deep sleep.

He squirmed as he started to have his recurring dream again. No, no, no! Again, at the same train station at dawn. Again, the same train. Again, Jimmy stood at the side door of the train. Only now, it was Jimmy as he was at the present, an adult. Again, in slow motion, silent, and sepia-toned, the steam train pulled out from the station. And again, a woman darted out from the station. Only now, it was Anita. She ran as hard as she could for the departing train car. But this time, she managed to catch up with it. Jimmy held onto a door handle as he reached out for her. Closer and closer. Their hands touched, then clasped. One final heave and Jimmy pulled her up onto the small stairs leading to the doorway. He pulled her in and closed the door. Anita was out of breath but smiling. They hugged, and then kissed. Jimmy, in his sleep, stopped squirming. A sense of peace and comfort washed over him as he smiled.

A BEATING AND
A HEALING

In his studio, Jimmy whistled while he shaved for the first time in three days. Using a straight razor with a bandaged hand did not seem like a good idea—he could imagine many cuts on his face. Before he started to mix up the shaving cream, he looked at his stubble of a beard and thought about growing it out. Nah, maybe another time.

Wearing a white shirt with high collar and a tie, he looked at the old vaudeville poster of 'Perry and Johnson' on the wall. Jimmy made a fateful decision that released a ton of baggage and guilt from his shoulders. He ripped the poster down and tossed it into a garbage can. He went to his dresser, picked up his mother's photo, looked at it one last time, and placed it in a drawer. He decided that Russell was right—that looking for their mother all this time was wasteful and futile. He would keep fond memories of her but he needed to spend his energies on the future, not the past. He had always berated his father for living too much in the past, for not embracing the here and now—trains instead of cars, vaudeville instead of moving pictures—only to realize that he too was guilty of that.

Looking in a mirror, he applied a small truncated stage moustache to his clean shaven face. He slipped on a coat that was too small and a derby hat which reminded him of his vaudeville days. He looked good, just like Charlie Chaplin. He looked at his clock which read 4 p.m. He'd best hurry. Out the door, he picked up a cane.

On the way to open this new chapter in his life, Jimmy walked into a flower shop and bought a bouquet. The store-keeper and passers-by snickered as they recognized who he was supposed to be. He put out a thumb to try to hitch a ride. A streetcar pulled up nearby and stopped. Passengers got on and off. Suddenly, he felt liberation from his phobia about trains. He walked over and got on. As the streetcar started up and ambled down the tracks, none of the fear and anxiety that used to grip him materialized.

At the stop near Prospect Printing, three ruffians, in their twenties, waited for the streetcar. They were loud, rowdy, and pushed each other around. Other passengers in waiting gave them a wide berth. The streetcar approached.

On board, Jimmy was entertaining the passengers with Chaplin mannerisms. Children were especially enthralled. The streetcar slowed down and stopped. Jimmy looked out to see if this was his stop. It was. He tipped his hat as he and other passengers got off.

Anita was leaving work. She noticed the streetcar as she turned to walk home.

Jimmy spotted her and raised his hand to get her attention. As he was about to call out her name, one of the ruffians stopped him. Talking to his mates, he said, "What is this? Charlie friggin' Chaplin?" His mates chuckled.

The second ruffian said, "Only, I ain't never seen no nigger Charlie Chaplin."

A third one agreed, "Me either."

Wanting no trouble, Jimmy tried to defuse the situation by doing some Chaplin mannerisms. They were not amused. Jimmy had no time for this and said, "Let's continue this later, blokes, maybe over a beer." Tipping his hat, he tried to go around them, and called out, "Anita!"

She looked into his direction, at first not seeing him but recognizing his voice. She whispered to herself, "Jimmy?"

The first ruffian said to Jimmy, "Oh, you think you're so funny. How about this for a laugh?" He threw a punch. Jimmy ducked in time but the second one landed a punch into Jimmy's stomach, making him fold over and drop the flowers. He then slowly stood up. Channeling heavyweight champion Jack Johnson, Jimmy marshaled his resources and squarely punched the mouth of the first ruffian. Surprised, and spitting out blood, the first ruffian got furious and tackled Jimmy to the ground. Now his other two mates were kicking a helpless Jimmy. Onlookers were stunned but were reluctant to get involved.

Anita ran towards the commotion, screaming, "Jimmy. Jimmy! Hey, stop. Stop it!" Suddenly, a figure bolted past her, got to the fight, and threw one of the ruffians away, then the second one. The final ruffian stood up and backed away. He didn't want any part of Henry still in his printing apron with his fists clenched.

A witness to the fight had summoned a nearby patrolman who blew his whistle. At the sight of the approaching patrolman, the ruffians ran to the streetcar as it was leaving and jumped on board just in time. The patrolman gave chase but could not catch them.

Jimmy, still on his back and seeing Henry and what he had done, said, "Hey, thanks, Henry." Henry smiled and then pulled Jimmy up, brushing dirt off his costume. He retrieved Jimmy's fallen derby. Anita arrived and exclaimed, "Jimmy! My, God. You're bleeding."

Jimmy tasted the trickle of blood from a corner of his mouth. Anita took out a handkerchief from her purse and wiped it away. His stage moustache was knocked half off. Anita pulled it off and handed it to him. He smiled at her. He then looked around and picked up the stepped on bouquet and handed it to Anita. He said, "These <u>were</u> for you." Looking at what was left of the mangled flowers, they both had to chuckle.

Henry said, "Come on in and wash up." The patrolman let matters be and went on his way.

At Echo Park Lake near his studio, Jimmy and Anita sat on a bench looking at ducks and boaters on the water. Jimmy had set his derby and cane down on the ground and was tossing pebbles into the lake.

Jimmy said, "I haven't had the chance to tell you but I lost my job."

Anita reacted with dismay, "Jimmy, no. How? Why?"

Jimmy chuckled, "You don't want to know. I know, and I don't want to know." Solemnly, he said, "I also gave up looking for my mother."

Anita looked at him in disbelief.

He continued, "I finally got it through my thick skull that Russell was right. Too many years have passed. I was just wasting my time, and George's."

She tried to explain, "That thing with George happened—"

He put a finger to her lips, and said, "I understand."

He showed her his blistered palm, finally healing. "And, I damned near ruined my hand diggin' ditches."

Anita, gently taking his injured hand, said with sympathy, "Oh, Jimmy, you don't have to dig ditches."

"Yeah, well, it's too bad I'm so fond of eating." He smiled, as did she.

He stood up, paced a bit, and continued, "And, I can't finish my picture—my actors moved to Philadelphia."

Anita shook her head in more disbelief.

He said, "I have to either start over with new actors, or pay for Blake and Rose to return. Where can I get that kind of money?" In anger, he slammed his right fist into his left palm. "Damn, that hurts!" Shaking off the pain in his injured hand, he said, "All that work wasted. I can't sell a picture that's not finished. Oh, what's the use? I'll just have to give that up too. Pop was right. I am a bum."

Anita protested, "Of course, you're not." She stood up pulling him up and then hugged him.

Jimmy gave a deep sigh and looked her in the eye, "But, the worst was I thought I lost you."

She smiled, caressed his face, and tried to kiss him. Except, one side of his lips was swollen and tender from the ruffian's beating.

He reacted, "Ouch. Not there."

She said, "Oh, sorry."

He indicated the other side of his mouth, "Here." She kissed him gingerly on the uninjured side. She suddenly broke away with a thought leaving him with his eyes closed and lips puckered.

Anita said, "Didn't you say that you only had a couple of scenes in your picture to do?"

Opening his eyes, he said, "Yes. And, that's what kills me. I was almost there!" He angrily picked up a rock and threw it into the lake for emphasis. A flock of ducks scattered, squawking.

She said, "Your brother Russell. He looks to be about the same height and build as Blake. If he puts on a beard, could he take Blake's part?"

Jimmy paced as he pondered the idea. "Not bad, not bad at all. But who—"

Anita had the answer, "With some makeup and a different hairstyle, I could take the place of Rose."

Jimmy looked at her, and imagined it. "You would do that?"

"Oh, yes!"

Jimmy raised his arms up in joy. "Anita, it's brilliant. You just saved my picture."

He twirled her around as she laughed.

Stopping, Jimmy said, "I love you."

She replied, "I love you."

They kissed again, long and hard. Grabbing her hand, he said, "Come on. Let's go find Russell."

They hurried across the park, leaving behind his derby and cane.

CHAPTER 25

JUST DESERTS

At the Roxie Theater, with piano music playing, Reed and Russell were in the middle of their performance before a near capacity crowd.

Outside, Jimmy and Anita ran up to the box office and bought two tickets. As they rushed in, Jimmy said, "I hope we haven't missed them."

In the darkened theater, they found two seats towards the back and sat down. They had made it just in time. Jimmy pointed to his father and brother on stage to Anita who smiled.

Also watching on an aisle seat, in the middle of the theater, was Edgar Perry. Watching and seething. He reached into a paper bag under his seat and took out a large ripe tomato. He stood up in the aisle and tossed the tomato toward the stage, hitting Reed on the chest. All in the audience and on stage were stunned. Some gasped. The piano player slowed down, and then stopped. Jimmy stood up to get a better look.

Edgar yelled in a clear voice, "Stealing my act, Reed Johnson?"

Bewildered, Reed wiped tomato juice from his suit. He peered at the man in the darkness. Recognizing this voice from his past, he asked, "Edgar? Edgar Perry, is that you?"

Jimmy whispered, "Can't be."

Edgar said, "Damn right, it is."

Russell was taking none of this, leaping off the stage and running toward Edgar.

Fearful, Edgar muttered, "Oh, shit," as he turned to run only to find Jimmy standing in his way. POW! Jimmy punched Edgar in the face, knocking him backwards. The audience applauded and cheered. It had been a long time since he was so heartily applauded. He forgot how good that felt.

Backstage, Sam was watching the next act warm up—a pair of magicians, one was juggling balls and the other one blowing out fire when Sam noticed that Reed's performance had ended prematurely. He asked, "Oh, what's going on now!?"

He looked on stage to see Reed in a slick of tomato juice, and Russell and Jimmy dragging Edgar up the aisle toward the stage. He pointed to the next act and said, "Yancy Brothers. You're on. NOW!"

The magicians unexpectedly had to hurry to gather their equipment and themselves. In their haste, their rabbit hopped away and escaped. The fire eater tried to chase her but his partner said, "Forget it. Come on." They hastily leapt onto the stage, set up, and started their act.

Sam led Reed and Anita to his office. Jimmy and Russell followed while dragging Edgar who was still unconscious. On the way, Jimmy introduced Anita to his father. Anita remarked, "How do you do? Not the way I thought we would meet." They smiled at each other.

In Sam's office, Jimmy and Russell sat Edgar into a chair. Jimmy tossed a cup of water into Edgar's face. He immediately revived, spitting out water. He could not quite focus as he tried to get up but Russell, behind him, pushed him back down. Edgar took stock of his situation, smiled, and said, "Evening, gents. And mi'lady." Anita did not return his toothless grin.

Reed barked, "What the hell, Edgar?"

Edgar sat up straight and shot back, "What the hell, yourself!" He paused, and then said, "The great Reed Johnson. Still playing to a packed house. I had to see it for myself. And look at me. I'm a bum, a bum playing in bars and dives. This is what you did to me, Reed—you and Miriam." This jolted Jimmy.

With fire in his eyes, Reed said, "You mean, <u>you</u> and Miriam, don't you?"

Edgar replied, "You and I were playing to packed houses and we could have played the big houses—"

Jimmy didn't care about that and said, "Stop!" He got into Edgar's face, and said, "What do you know about Miriam?"

"Who the hell are you?"

"Jimmy, Reed's son."

Edgar had to laugh and put his hand level about two feet off the floor. "Little Jimmy Johnson! My God." He looked behind him, "And, you are—"

"Russell."

Edgar chuckled again. He looked at his old partner and said, "Damn, Reed, how time flies—"

Jimmy interrupted, "Answer the question, dammit! Where is our mother!?"

Edgar suddenly got serious and said, "Miriam? How in blazes should I know?"

Reed got into Edgar's face, and said, "Bastard! You took her away. That night, you brought me her slip. You wrote that note—"

Russell was shocked, and said, "Her slip?"

Jimmy asked, "What note?"

Reed took a deep breath, and said, "Sorry, boys. I never wanted you to know—"

Jimmy said, "Pop, we need to know. Please, tell us what happened. Russell and I have the right."

Reed sighed in resignation, "Yes, you do. You do have the right."

THE TRUTH
COMES OUT

Reed gathered his thoughts and began his story: "Twenty-five years ago, Edgar and I were vaudeville partners when we met Miriam on the Circuit..."

He told them how he and Miriam fell in love despite Edgar's concurrent and desperate pursuit of Miriam. He told how he and Miriam decided to marry, how he broke off the act with Edgar to start a new one with Miriam. He told of the last time he had seen Edgar, on their wedding day. He told of Jimmy and Russell being born and introduced into the act.

Finally, he got to the night that Jimmy would visit in his dreams all these years. 'The Family Johnson' had just finished their act and taken their bows. Although it went very well, with thunderous applause from the audience, Miriam left the stage unhappy. With the audience applauding for more, Reed brought his boys back out for a curtain call. He looked for Miriam but she had already headed for the dressing room.

Back in their hotel room, Miriam tucked the boys in for the night. She turned the gas lights off, and quietly closed the door. Three-year-old Russell fell right to sleep. Five-year-old Jimmy, tired but hyped up by the evening's performance, heard his parents' voices—angry voices—from the other room. He sat up and went to the door, cracking it open slightly to listen.

In the main room, Reed had his shoes off, coat off, vest open, and was holding a drink. He said, "Miriam, let's call it a night. We are both tired. We can talk about this tomorrow."

She said angrily, "You always want to talk about it tomorrow but tomorrow comes and nothing comes of it. I think I've made my position clear—I don't want the boys in the act anymore."

Reed jumped up, and said, "Didn't you hear that audience tonight, Miriam? They love the boys. I tell you, we got a gold mine here."

"I want us to settle down, stay in one town. Stop traveling from one hotel to another. Give the boys a proper schooling. I want them to learn to read and write."

Reed, getting frustrated, said, "I ain't never had proper schooling. And I'm doing all right. Besides, what do you want me to do? I can't do nothin' but dance."

"Your father ran a barber shop. Maybe you could too."

"Me? Cutting hair!?"

Reed put both of his hands around his neck, made a pretend choking sound, and fell to the ground. Jimmy thought this was funny and smiled.

Miriam was not amused, and said, "That's not going to work this time."

Reed got up, picked up his glass and took another sip. He said, "Come on, Miriam, be serious."

She finally revealed what she had been thinking for a long time, and said, "I'm wanting to take the boys to my mother's and move in with her."

Reed did a slow burn. The glass in his hand shook, whiskey splashing out. Suddenly, he threw his glass against the wall, smashing it to bits, leaving a wet spot on the wallpaper. This caused Miriam to jump and Jimmy to shudder. He was fearful.

Reed retorted, "Like hell you are, Miriam!! You ain't never taking my boys away. Hear me!!" He ran up to her with a raised open hand as if he was going to strike her. She cowered. Jimmy winced. Reed put his hand down.

Miriam recovered and picked up her purse. Angrily, she said, "I'm getting out of here. But this is not the end of it, Reed Johnson!" She opened, and then slammed the door. He locked it, and kicked it.

Jimmy slowly closed the bedroom door and crawled back to bed, tears rolling down his cheeks. He looked over at Russell, still blissfully sleeping.

Miriam emerged from their hotel upset. She stopped to collect herself, taking out a handkerchief and wiping away tears. She heard her name, "Miriam?" Startled, she looked up and saw Edgar. She was relieved it was not Reed, but she wasn't especially happy to see Edgar. She said, "Edgar Perry! What are you doing here?"

"I'm working just down the street."

She started to walk away but then turned to say, "I still haven't forgiven you for ruining my wedding day."

Edgar said, "Uh, well, I do apologize. I just went a little crazy. I lost my best friend, and I lost the best girl I ever met."

She smiled. He then put a comforting arm around her, and said, "Now, tell me what's the matter, missy. What are you doing out here this time of night?"

She said, "That husband of mine can be so unreasonable sometimes."

Edgar sensed an opportunity, and said, "Oh, don't I know. He can be such an ass— Come on, tell me about it." He escorted her away.

He took her to a local tavern where he bought two mugs of beer. He took a big sip but she was hesitant. He said, "Go on, take a drink. It will make you feel better."

She said, "Oh, you know I'm no good with alcohol." Then, defiantly, she picked up her mug. "Oh, what the hell? One can't hurt."

Later that evening, Miriam was working on her third or fourth beer—who was counting? Several empty mugs filled their table. Suddenly, she burped loudly. She was embarrassed but this caused the both of them to laugh hysterically.

She said, "Oh, Edgar. If only things were different." She touched his hand. "Thank you. But I need to get home and face the music." She tried to get up, got tipsy and started to fall.

Edgar caught her. He said, "Careful, mi'lady. Let me get you home."

She passed out. He heaved her over a shoulder. Smiling, he slapped her on the behind. The bar crowd whooped and hollered as they left.

❖ ❖ ❖

I n the first light of the morning, in bed next to her man, Miriam slowly awakened. She found herself undressed. She touched the man next to her, also undressed, his back to her. She said, "Reed, I'm so sorry about last night—"

When the man turned over, she saw that it wasn't Reed. It was Edgar! Shocked, she looked about the room, and realized it was not their hotel room. She screamed. This woke up Edgar, groggy. He said, "Good morning, darling."

Miriam was in disbelief, and sputtered, "What... What am I doing here!?"

"Oh, you were simply magnificent. I can now die a happy man."

She screamed again, got up, picked up articles of her clothing, and hastily got dressed. She was in a panic, saying, "What have you done? What have we done? And, where is my slip?"

Edgar just yawned and turned over. Not concerned, he said, "Somewhere. I'm sure."

D awn was breaking as Miriam ran down the mostly empty streets toward her hotel. A few horse-drawn carts and people bundled up against the cold were out starting their day. She came upon her hotel and ran in, past a yawning desk clerk who looked up in surprise from his morning coffee, and ran up the stairs.

At their room, she stopped and took some deep breaths to calm down. She took out her key and as quietly as she could, unlocked the door. She took off her shoes and tip-toed in. The living room was dark but their bedroom door was open with a light on. "Dammit," she thought, "Reed was up already—he never gets up this early after an evening show." She slowly closed the front door and took another deep breath to face her husband. As she went into their bedroom, she started to say, "Reed, I can explain—"

Their bedroom was empty! Shocked, she dropped her shoes. She found the closet open and his clothes gone. Empty hangars were strewn on the floor. Empty dresser drawers were left open. A couple of her dresses on hangars were on the floor but for the most part her clothes were still in the closet as well as in the drawers. In a panic, she ran to the boys' bedroom. The boys were gone too with their dresser drawers and closet empty. She screamed, "No!" as she breathed hard, now scared.

She hurried back into the living room and turned on the light, trying to collect her thoughts when she found her slip and a handwritten note on an end table. Reading it, she could only shake her head in disbelief, saying, "Dammit! Dammit!"

She dropped the note, hastily put on her shoes, and ran out, leaving the door open.

The handwritten note read, "Reed, you've lost. Miriam's with me now. As it should be. (Signed) Edgar."

Miriam rushed to the hotel desk clerk. Almost out of breath, she inquired, "Did Mr. Johnson in 204 come through here with two small boys?"

"Yes, ma'am, he did. About two hours ago. I think they were headed to the train station—"

She dashed out. He finished her thought, "You're welcome."

In the waiting room of the train station, Miriam looked around desperately. She did not see her family and rushed to the train clerk. He told her that a man with two small boys did get on the train, and it was about to leave. They heard the train whistle. She ran out the gate.

The clerk yelled out, "Lady, wait! You'll need to buy a ticket—"

As in Jimmy's dream, the steam train with Reed, Jimmy, and Russell pulled away. At the side door of the train, Jimmy looked out, hoping against hope. Then he saw his mother running towards the train. She saw him too for a fleeting moment.

But, it was too late. The train gained too much speed and put too much distance between them. Miriam realized she could not catch up with it. She slowed down, and then stopped, falling behind some crates with her back to the departing train. She was crying uncontrollably.

Inside the train car, Reed had pulled his son back inside who was pleading, "Pop, make them stop the train. It's Mom. Make them stop."

When Reed looked out the door, he did not see anyone at the receding station. He pulled his son back to their seat and said, "Come on, son. You're mistaken. There's no one there."

At their seat, Russell was asleep, wrapped in a blanket. Jimmy, not understanding, nevertheless stopped crying. Reed wiped away his tears. He said, "It will be all right, son. It will be all right." When Jimmy found the tintype of his mother in his suitcase, he knew that it wouldn't be.

In Sam's office, all eyes were on Edgar. Jimmy said, "Well, Edgar..."

Edgar, squirming in his chair, confirmed, "Yeah, that's pretty much it. Except for one thing—nothing happened between Miriam and me that night. I mean, we slept in the same bed but that's all we did. I let Miriam and Reed think different." He smiled slyly, "You see, I am a gentleman."

With rage in his eyes, Reed lunged at Edgar, saying, "You stupid idiot!"

Edgar cringed for the onslaught but Jimmy and Russell held Reed back. Reed composed himself and shook them off.

Jimmy put his face inches from Edgar's, and demanded, "What happened to our mother!? Tell us the truth—"

Russell stepped in and held up a fist, "Or the next time we won't hold him back."

Edgar laughed nervously, "Hold it, gents." He held up his right hand, and said, "I swear on a stack of Bibles. After Miriam left my place, I ain't never seen her again—to this day."

"Liar!" Reed shouted.

Edgar looked Reed in the eye, "And, I'm telling you—it's the God honest truth!"

Jimmy backed away from Edgar. He looked at his father, "You see, Pop, I told you. I did see Mom at the station that morning."

Edgar felt vindicated, pointing to Jimmy, "You see, there you go. There's the truth."

Reed had to entertain the possibility that Jimmy was right and that he had made a huge mistake. "Damn." He looked at his sons, and tried to make amends, "Boys, if Edgar is telling the truth—" He scowled at his old partner, "...and I ain't sayin' he is."

Edgar quickly shot up his right hand again.

Reed looked at his sons, "But if so, then I am truly sorry. But what was I to think? Edgar fooled me and your mother both."

This time, Reed could not hold back his anger. He jumped on Edgar, yelling, "You bastard!"

Edgar screamed as his chair fell backwards and the two former partners scuffled. Before Jimmy or Russell could react, there was a hard knocking on the door as a panicked stagehand threw open the door and black smoke poured in. He screamed, "Boss, better get out here! The fire eater's got the curtain on fire."

Reed was poised to hit Edgar one more time when Sam cursed, "Oh, shit," as he ran out the door. The others all followed.

Sam, Jimmy, Anita, Reed, Russell, the fire eater, the juggler, and stage hands formed a bucket brigade and were dousing the burning curtain with water. Remaining audience members screamed as they pushed out in a panic.

Outside, a horse drawn fire engine pulled up. Fire fighters struggled to get in with their hose as people emptied the theater, including Edgar, battered and bruised, who disappeared into the night.

Reed started coughing. He wobbled and couldn't grab the bucket Jimmy was passing. Russell grabbed it instead and ordered, "Jimmy and Anita, get Pop out of here!"

Jimmy and Anita led Reed by his arms down the stage steps and up the aisle as fire fighters ran past them. The lead fireman opened the nozzle and hit the flames with water.

Outside, Jimmy and Anita led Reed, still coughing, to the curb and sat him down. Jimmy gently patted Reed on the back, "Pop, you're going to be okay. You're going to be okay." He was reassuring himself as much as his father.

Indeed, out in the cool smoke free air, the coughing slowed down, then stopped. Reed started breathing normally again and panic left his face. He then looked deeply into Jimmy's eyes for the first time in a long time. He remembered what his mother said to him at his dad's funeral, how each person needed to find their own way, then started crying. Alarmed, Jimmy asked, "Pop, what's the matter? Does something hurt?"

Reed tapped his chest, and said, "No, no, son. In here. I hurt inside for what I did to you. What kind of father would do that to their own son? I don't expect you to ever forgive me." Then Reed reached into his pocket and fished out his father's pocket watch, the one that Jimmy tried to fix so many years before. He caressed it one last time, and then handed it to Jimmy, saying, "Here, take it."

Jimmy was astonished, and said, "Pop, that's grandpa's watch."

Reed broke down in tears. "I know. You're my first born. I... I want you to have it."

Hesitatingly, Jimmy took it, popped open the cover, and watched the second hand circle around. He started to tear up as he pulled his father close to him, and said, "All right, Pop, all right." Jimmy showed the watch to Anita who smiled, holding back tears.

Russell ran out of the theater and called out, "Jimmy. Pop!"

They turned to see him and all stood up. Jimmy yelled out, "Here!" Anita took Jimmy's hand.

Russell rushed over with much concern. Looking Reed in the eye and seeing tears, he asked, "Pop, are you all right?"

Reed smiled and hugged both of his sons, one with each arm. "I'm good, more than good..." Russell understood and smiled at Jimmy who smiled back.

CHAPTER 27

UNPLEASANT DECISION

At La Grande train station in downtown Los Angeles where Jimmy and his father and brother first arrived in the city, a small crowd of waiting passengers watched as Jimmy prepared a scene. He had set up his camera on a tripod, and then held up a mirror so that Russell could attach a stage beard to match Blake's face. Russell also wore clothes similar to what Blake had been wearing in Jimmy's movie. Anita likewise was dressed and made up like Rose. Jimmy then got behind his camera.

Jimmy said, "Ready, Russell?"

Russell looked at the camera and moved into position. He asked, "Where do you want me? Here?"

Jimmy said, "That's fine. Okay, Anita, stand next to Russell. Here we go."

Anita moved into the scene. Jimmy said, "Okay, in this last scene, Russell, you have caught Anita before she could leave town. You two have realized that you can't live without each other and have made up." Jimmy started cranking the camera and took a breath. He said, "I can't believe I'm saying this, but Russell, go ahead and kiss Anita."

Russell and Anita looked lovingly into each other's eyes. He caressed her cheek. They embraced and then kissed.

"Beautiful," Jimmy said as he slowly closed the camera iris, and then stopped cranking. "Iris down. Done. Finished." Jimmy looked up to see Russell and Anita still kissing. "All right, you two, knock it off!"

Russell and Anita broke it off laughing as some in the crowd applauded. Russell said, "Man, I really like this moving picture acting. You sure you don't want a do over of this kissing scene?"

Jimmy was smiling as he said, "I got it. It's fine!"

Russell took off his beard. Jimmy went over to the couple and got between them, giving them both a hug. The crowd started to disperse. Jimmy said, "Thanks, you two. Now, where to get the money to get this film processed, now that I can't use Sunset Camera?" He released them to ponder his options. He looked at Russell, and started to ask, "Hey, buddy, old pal, old friend of mine—"

Russell was quick to react, "Oh, no. You still owe me fifty bucks."

Anita begged, "You're not going to dig more ditches, are you?"

Jimmy shoved his hand under his arm and grimaced. Russell had an idea, and suggested, "I know Pop would welcome you back into the act." Jimmy grimaced even more. He took a deep breath and realized what he had to do. He said, "Oh, crap."

The next day, he went to Madame's apartment and knocked on her door.

FATEFUL DISCOVERY

At Griffith's studio, Madame and Jimmy approached the front door of the barn. Extras, in Babylonian costumes, emerged from the barn and passed them on their way to the set. Jimmy studied them intently as they walked by, searching for any reason to turn around and leave. He still had an uneasy feeling about this.

Jimmy said, "I'm telling you, Madame, if I see anyone here in blackface, I'm getting the hell out!"

"Not to worry, honey."

They walked into the massive dressing room. The place was abuzz as many dressers feverishly worked on many extras. At first, Jimmy couldn't help but be awestruck.

Madame said, "I have my big scene today. Kinda nervous." She saw the costume boss, and yelled out, "Sophie, we're here."

Sophie waved them over. Madame said, "Sophie, this is Jimmy, the guy I told you about."

Sophie, with a dozen things on her mind, had straight pins in her mouth while adjusting a costume. She searched her memory, and said through the pins, "Remind me again."

"He fans the auction guy."

Sophie muffled, "Oh, right."

Jimmy was taken aback, "What? I thought you said I could be an Ethiopian king."

Madame said, "Just like my babies, you got to crawl before you can run. Just keep thinking to yourself, five dollars a day, five dollars a day."

Taking out the pins, Sophie looked about the room, and yelled out, "Doris!" Doris looked up. Sophie pointed to Jimmy. "He fans the Auctioneer."

Doris nodded, and then waved Jimmy over.

Sophie took out Madame's costume off a rack and told Madame, "Here, have Helen help you."

Madame took her costume, and called out, "Helen!"

Helen waved to Madame. Unwittingly, Jimmy passed his mother to reach Doris. They exchanged brief glances but with the passing of so many years, neither recognized the other.

O n the set of the Marriage Market scene, Griffith consulted with his main actors, the Mountain Girl, the Auctioneer, and the Babylonian king, Belshazzar, as his assistants got the extras into their positions. Griffith looked around and didn't see Madame. He motioned to Karl, and said, "Find out what's keeping Nellie."

"Yes, sir." He took off running.

In the scene that Griffith envisioned, the Auctioneer sold young maidens to prospective buyers—older men of wealth. The Mountain Girl, a feisty rough and tumble young woman in goat skin garb who ate raw green onions, was supposed to be auctioned also. She protested. Since she had earlier fought a battle for Belshazzar, when Belshazzar showed up, he granted her marriage amnesty so that she could choose to marry whomever she wanted.

In the middle of the set was a large elevated stand, the auction platform with steps without handrails leading up to it. A smaller platform to the side was where the Auctioneer did his work. Prospective maidens sat at the foot of the platform, nervously waiting to be sold. Madame's role was to escort the maidens one by one to the auction platform while Jimmy was to simply wave a large fan over the Auctioneer.

Back in the dressing room, Helen put the final touches on Madame's costume. Right next to her, Doris fitted Jimmy. He was bare-chested except for strands of beads. He had on African-decorated shorts and sandals. Doris handed him a large ostrich feather fan. Jimmy and Helen worked nearly side by side, oblivious to each other.

Karl appeared at the front door and yelled out, "Madame, and anyone else for the Marriage Market, let's move! We're ready."

Madame looked at Jimmy. She couldn't help but smirk, destroying any confidence that he had. She reminded him, "Keep thinking, five dollars a day, five dollars a day."

As they walked out, Jimmy, under his breath, did so.

Jimmy's uneasiness stopped when they stepped onto the Marriage Market set. Jimmy stared at the scene before him, an open air set with twenty-foot walls painted in Babylonian style, three dozen actors and extras, a half dozen crew, all under the deft control of Griffith. Way in the back of his mind, he could not help but admire the skill with which Griffith kept all of these moving parts going at once. He also thought of the money he had to struggle to scrape together over this past year just to make his one little photoplay. What hundreds, thousands, even millions of dollars were being spent here? Somehow, it just didn't seem fair. Then he spotted the man himself. He felt a lurching in his gut. He thought, "This is wrong. How could I be working for such a bastard—"

Suddenly, a crew member ushered Jimmy into his position and gave him instructions, basically to wave his ostrich feathers fan up and down slowly near the Auctioneer who was waiting for the first girl to perch on the auction platform. Madame went to Griffith to get her final instructions. Warmly, Griffith greeted her, and demonstrated her actions on the auction platform. She understood, and took her position at the bottom of the stairs. The First Young Maiden to be auctioned stood up and joined her. Jimmy couldn't understand how Madame could have such a cordial relationship with the man he hated so much. He just wanted to punch him in the nose. With a clenched jaw, he thought, "I'll do this today but I won't be back tomorrow. If need be, I'll go back to digging ditches."

Griffith nodded to Slocum who blew a whistle to get everyone's attention. Slocum yelled, "All right, ladies and gentlemen, we are about to shoot the scene. You have your instructions."

Griffith asked his cameraman, "Ready, Billy?"

"Ready, sir." Billy started cranking his camera.

Griffth barked, "Fade in!"

He watched Madame take the First Young Maiden up the stairs to the platform and showed her to would-be buyers. At first, Jimmy dutifully fanned the Auctioneer as the Auctioneer conducted the auction and got bids. But Jimmy was distracted and getting angrier and angrier as he watched Griffith shouting out commands from his chair. Oops. Jimmy accidentally hit the Auctioneer in the face with the fan feathers who sneezed loudly. Some extras stopped to laugh. Griffith saw this and was not happy. He said, "Stop. Stop!"

All action stopped. Billy stopped the camera. All looked at Griffith. Griffith turned to his assistant and indicated Jimmy, "Karl, who is that kid, that boy?"

Karl shrugged, "Someone Madame brought in."

Griffith stood up and looked at Jimmy. In a loud voice, he said, "Hey, you. Boy! Next time, pay attention—"

At first, Jimmy didn't know that Griffith was talking to him. He pointed to himself quizzically.

Griffith said, "Yes, you. Watch—"

Jimmy stopped waving the fan, and said in a loud, clear voice, "Did you call me... boy?" That's it! Before Griffith could answer, Jimmy dropped the fan, and walked off, ripping off the beads. To Griffith, Jimmy angrily and loudly said, "Nobody calls me that, especially not the likes of you!"

Griffith was taken aback by this insurrection, as was Madame and the others in the cast and crew. Madame ran down the steps to confront Jimmy. She said, "Jimmy, what in God's name are you doing?"

"Sorry, Madame. I knew this was a mistake," Jimmy said as he walked off the set.

Griffith said to Madame, "Nellie, bring him back or we'll find someone else. We don't have all afternoon."

"Yes, Mr. Griffith." Madame was furious as she chased after Jimmy.

Back at the barn, the dressers were taking a well deserved break, readying themselves for when the scene was over and the cast and extras came back *en masse*. They were surprised when Jimmy came back so soon with Madame following.

Sophie asked, "Is the scene over already?"

Jimmy said angrily, "It is for me. Where are my clothes?" He rifled through racks of clothing. "Where are my clothes, I said!"

Doris, confused, jumped up, found them, and said, "Here they are." Other dressers, including Helen, took notice.

Madame spun Jimmy around as he got dressed out in the open. She said, "Hey! What the hell are you doing? I thought you were crackerjack."

Jimmy said, "Madame, what <u>are</u> we doing?" Pointing in the direction of the set, he reminded, "Our kinfolk were sold in auctions like that!"

This momentarily stopped Madame who struggled to reconcile, "No, this... this be a marriage market..."

"Same thing, Madame, same thing. What was I thinking, coming here?"

Sophie came over, as did some of the other dressers, including Helen. Griffith and Slocum marched in as Jimmy finished getting dressed.

Griffith said, "Nellie, come back to the set. We need you to finish this today. We got someone else to wave the fan. We won't need him." Griffith pointed to Jimmy.

Jimmy got into Griffith's face, said, "That's right. You don't need me. You never needed <u>any</u> of us!"

Jimmy turned to Madame, and said, "Madame, Nellie, whatever hell you call yourself, how can you work for this... this cretin?"

Madame slapped Jimmy, "Apologize to Mr. Griffith." The slap shocked many in the room. Griffith looked bemused.

Jimmy stood his ground, and said, "What for?" He pointed a finger at Griffith, and said, "You're the reason I'm making moving pictures. Pictures that <u>you</u> will never make—"

"Wait. You're making moving pictures?"

"What the hell? Do you think you're the only one who can pick up a camera?"

"No, of course not, but— Well, that's impressive. But I still want you off my lot."

"Gladly."

Through all this, Helen shook her head at this incident, wondering how anyone could be so fired-up angry at Griffith. Unconsciously, she touched her locket.

Griffith said to his burly assistant, "Mr. Slocum, kindly show this boy—I mean, this young man—out."

Slocum said, "With pleasure," as he took Jimmy's arm and started to escort him out.

Jimmy shook off Slocum's grasp, and said defiantly, "I know my own way out! No one shows James Reed Johnson the door! Good-bye!!"

Helen had her back turned, tending to some fabric. When she heard Jimmy shout out his full name, a bolt of electricity shot through her body just as sure as if she touched a live wire. She quickly spun around and looked at this brash young man opening the front door. She started to breathe heavily, staring.

Could it be? Just as Jimmy was about to step out of her life, Helen broke the silence in an anguished voice, "J. J.!"

This stopped Jimmy in his tracks, as it did everyone. Jimmy turned around to face her. At first he was still angry, and said, "Hey! No one's called me that except..." Now, in a rush of realization and in a softer voice, "My... mother..."

Madame sucked in a quick breath as this connection finally dawned on her. She looked back and forth at the two people and shook her head wondering how she missed it.

Jimmy stared at Helen, trying to put together what was happening. She started to tear up. Jimmy walked slowly toward her. There was not a sound in the dressing room as all eyes were on Jimmy and Helen. Doris accidentally dropped a straight pin which pinged on the floor. When Jimmy got to Helen, she opened the locket to reveal the photos.

Jimmy couldn't believe it. He said, in a cracking voice, "That... that's me... and Russell!" He looked at Helen intently, finally recognizing her face from the tintype. She had the same eyes, the same mouth. He gently caressed her cheek. He said, "Mom," and gave her a big hug, now sobbing. Helen slowly put her arms around this stranger, and said, "J. J. My son."

Madame wiped away a tear. She walked up to them, and gave Jimmy a pat on the back, and hugged Helen.

Griffith said, "All right, before we all start blubbering, let's go make a picture." He said to Slocum in a quiet voice, "Give him a little time. And make sure he gets paid for today." Slocum looked at him quizzically. "You sure?"

"He's Helen's son."

Slocum didn't want to quarrel with the boss but if it were up to him... He simply nodded, and said, "Okay."

Griffith said, "Nellie. Come." Madame at first hesitated as she watched the mother and son reunion. Finally, she turned and followed Griffith out. Slocum sat down on a chair to wait. Jimmy took Helen by the hand and they sat down. Some of the other dressers started to draw close but Sophie shooed them away, allowing Jimmy and Helen some private time.

Jimmy was confused and said, "I don't understand. You're uh... Helen? My mother's name is Miriam."

"Helen is my middle name. After that terrible morning, I had to start a new life—"

Jimmy said, "I have so many questions—"

Helen placed a hand on his mouth, "So do I but not here."

CHAPTER 29

WHOLE AGAIN

Anita and Jimmy were busy making sandwiches for lunch. Helen was standing by Jimmy's workbench as she looked around in amazement inside the studio. She smiled and said to him, "You've really made something of yourself, J. J. Look at all this. I am so proud of you."

Jimmy said, "Wait until you see Russell and Anita in my picture."

Helen smiled, "I'm anxious to see them. I was in a couple of moving pictures myself—"

Jimmy looked up, "What!"

She waved her hand in dismissal. "Oh, it was nothing. I was a face in the crowd in a couple of Biograph flickers back in New York—"

Jimmy wiped his hands on a towel and said, "Speaking of New York..." He went to his dresser drawer and retrieved her tintype photo and showed it to her. She stared at it, momentarily lost in her thoughts, and then said, "Oh, my, look at me back then. Despite your father's grumblings that day, I still have fond memories our time at Coney Island." She started to cry.

"Mom, what's the matter?"

Setting the photo down, she said, "I'm sorry, but when I think of what Edgar and your father did to me... to us. For so long, I felt so ashamed."

Jimmy took his mother by the shoulders and looked into her eye, and said, "Mom, you have nothing to be ashamed of. You did nothing wrong except maybe trusting that good-for-nothing Edgar. He's out of our lives now. Russell and I will see to that."

Anita came over and said, "Helen, we're all here for you."

Jimmy released Helen who smiled and said to Anita, "Thank you, dear." Suddenly, Helen steeled herself and pounded Jimmy's workbench with her fist, rattling some tools. "You're right, dammit!" This surprised Jimmy and Anita. Jimmy had never heard his mother swear before.

Helen paced as she spoke, "I <u>didn't</u> do anything wrong. So, why should I keep beating myself up? You know what? Call me, 'Miriam.' It's the name my mother gave me. I'm taking it back." Miriam took a deep breath, finding new strength. Looking at Jimmy, she said, "I'm ready now to see your father."

She smiled and said, "Now, where's that lunch? I'm starving." They all laughed and headed towards the table.

Outside, George pulled up and parked his Lambert with the top down. Russell was sitting in the front seat while Reed sat in the middle of the back seat with his arms outstretched over the top of the upholstery.

Reed said, "George, this is what I call 'riding in style.' Russell, what's this about?"

Russell got out, shutting the door. "I don't know. Jimmy said he had a surprise and he wanted all three of us to come. Maybe his picture's done. Don't you want to see me act in my first movie?"

"Like Charlie Chaplin?"

Russell smiled, "Yes, like Charlie Chaplin."

Russell knocked on the door. Jimmy opened it. They all went in and Jimmy closed the door.

Two weeks later, in the darkened Roxie Theater, Jimmy's finished picture was playing on the big screen with piano accompaniment. Jimmy, Anita, Russell, Miriam, and Reed sat together watching. Miriam sat between her sons. Watching the final scenes featuring Anita and Russell, Russell pointed himself out to his mother who smiled while she held both Russell and Jimmy's hands. She couldn't have been happier.

Outside the theater, amid hand shakes and congratulatory back slapping, Jimmy remembered something. He dug out his wallet, took out a fifty-dollar bill and handed it to Russell who was pleasantly surprised.

EPILOGUE

Jimmy and Anita got married and soon made Miriam and Reed proud grandparents. Jimmy struggled to finish one more picture but like so many black independent filmmakers he could not achieve financial success. With a wife and baby to support, he sought and got his old job back at Sunset Camera. He eventually became the manager, then owner of the shop.

Miriam and Reed got a formal divorce but both remained in Los Angeles. Miriam continued to work in costumes in the movie industry while Reed and Russell gave up vaudeville. Reed worked in a barber shop near the Roxie Theater.

With Noble Johnson's help, **Russell** became an actor in Hollywood movies, eventually working in television in the early 1950s.

Edgar Perry died alone in an alley. He was buried in a pauper's grave. The exact date of his death and site of his grave are unknown.

Madame Sul-te-wan continued to work as an actress in Hollywood until the late 1950s, appearing in over forty films, notably opposite Claudette Colbert in *Maid of Salem*.

Noble Johnson and the Lincoln Motion Picture Company made four moving pictures for a predominately Negro audience before going out of business. Noble continued to work in Hollywood as an actor into the 1950s. Appearing in over 140 movies, besides playing the native chief in the original version of *King Kong*, Johnson worked with notables like Rudolph Valentino, John Barrymore, Frank Capra, and John Ford.

Oscar Micheaux wouldn't sell the motion picture rights to his first book to the Lincoln Motion Picture Company unless he directed. Knowing that he hadn't directed a movie before, they refused. Instead, Micheaux formed his own motion picture company in the Midwest, and made the picture himself. He did what Jimmy and Noble Johnson sought to do and made over forty films for the Negro community in thirty years, including musicals, comedies, Westerns, romances, and gangster films. His *Within Our Gates* was a direct repudiation of *The Birth of a Nation*.

With the financial failure of *Intolerance*, **D. W. Griffith's** power as a filmmaker diminished. In 1948, he died almost a forgotten man in Hollywood, a town some say he invented.

Jimmy never forgot his early filmmaking days and always wondered what might have been. After World War II, he and Russell put together a retrospective that included his two movies and representative films of Madame Sul-te-wan, Noble Johnson, and Oscar Micheaux at the Roxie Theater.

ACKNOWLEDGMENTS

I would like to thank those who read the first draft of this work and offered their encouragement and advice:

First of all, to my good friend since our college days (yeah, chemistry class), writer Mel Gilden, who first suggested that I turn my original screenplay of this story into a novel, and for finding a zillion grammatical errors in his meticulous reading of the manuscript;

To Douglas Hergert, Gina Gotsill, Liz Miller, and Alliene Turner for their kind words and corrections;

To Tia Clausen and Fox for their enthusiastic support;

To members of the East Bay Chapter of the Society of Technical Communication who listened to my first public reading of a chapter and wanted to know when the book was coming out;

To Hizuru Cruz, graphic designer extraordinaire, who came up with numerous ideas for the cover including the one that adorns this book;

And, to Paul W. Cooper and Donald Bogle for their insight and inspiration.

Thank you all.

ABOUT THE AUTHOR

Joseph M. Humbert comes from a technical background. Educated in physics and technical communication, he has worked in a number of positions, including managing data processing, creating technical documentation, building Web sites, and starting and running an educational software company. He has written or co-written a play and several screenplays. He has a love of the movies and of history. *There's the Rub*, his first novel, combined these two passions. He and his wife live in Oakland, California and have two grown sons.

Made in the USA
Charleston, SC
27 October 2013